The First Time I Saw You
Copyright © 2018 Lorhainne Ekelund
Editor: Talia Leduc

ISBN-13: 978-1-990590-12-2

Give feedback on the book at:
lorhainneeckhart@hotmail.com

Twitter: @LEckhart
Facebook: AuthorLorhainneEckhart

Printed in the U.S.A

THE FIRST TIME I SAW YOU

The Friessens

LORHAINNE ECKHART

The First Time I Saw You

Like his parents, Andy and Laura Friessen, Gabriel knows what it means to face an impossible situation. When he puts up an ad looking for a roommate, he never expects to meet a down-on-her-luck gorgeous single mom with a meddling family, a crazy ex-boyfriend, and enough chemistry between them to heat the county. The only problem is that she doesn't believe in happily ever after and sees falling in love as a mistake only fools make. But Gabriel can't stop thinking about her, wanting her, and is determined to show her that the road to love isn't as dangerous as she believes.

Runaway (Andy and Laura)
Overdue
The Unexpected Storm (Neil and Candy)
The Wedding (Neil and Candy)

The Friessens: A New Beginning

The Deadline (Andy and Laura)
The Price to Love (Neil and Candy)
A Different Kind of Love (Brad and Emily)
A Vow of Love, A Friessen Family Christmas

The Friessens

The Reunion
The Bloodline (Andy & Laura)
The Promise (Diana & Jed)
The Business Plan (Neil & Candy)
The Decision (Brad & Emily)
First Love (Katy)
Family First
Leave the Light On
In the Moment
In the Family: A Friessen Family Christmas
In the Silence
In the Stars
In the Charm
Unexpected Consequences
It Was Always You
The First Time I Saw You
Welcome to My Arms
Welcome to Boston
I'll Always Love You
Ground Rules

A Reason to Breathe
You Are My Everything
Anything For You
The Homecoming includes FREE short story When They
Were Young
Stay Away From My Daughter
The Bad Boy
A Place to Call Our Own
The Visitor
All About Devon
Long Past Dawn
How to Heal a Heart
Keep Me In Your Heart

Want to know how all the series are linked? Stop by my blog for all the details: http://www.lorhainneeckhart.com/what-is-the-reading-order-of-your-books/

Now Available at a specially reduced price, The Friessen Legacy Collections:

1) The Outsider Series: The Complete Omnibus Collection
2) The Friessens A New Beginning: The Collection
3) The Friessens Books 1 - 5 Box Set
4) The Friessens Books 6 -8
5) The Friessen Books 9 - 11
6) The Friessen Books 12 - 14
7) The Friessen Books 15 - 18
8) The Friessen Books 19 -21
9. The Friessen Books 22 - 24
10) The Friessens Books 25 - 27
11) The Friessens Books 28 - 31

The Friessen Family

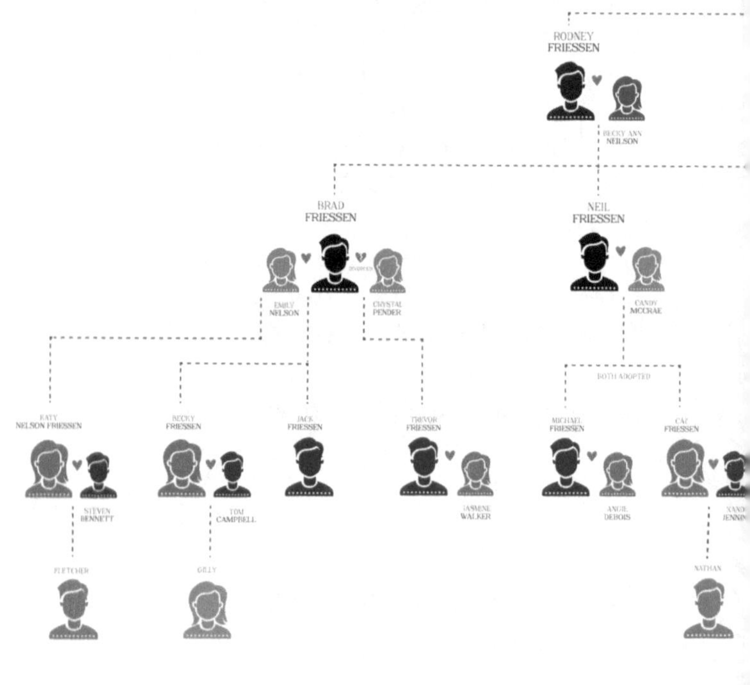

The Outsider Series

THE FORGOTTEN CHILD	BRAD & EMILY
A BABY AND A WEDDING	BRAD & EMILY & and and Neil Nielsen & Becky
FALLEN HERO	JED, DIANA & ANDY
THE SEARCH	JED, DIANA & ANDY
THE AWAKENING	ANDY & LAURA

The Outsider Series

SECRETS	DIANA & JED with the entire Friessen Family
RUNAWAY	ANDY & LAURA
OVERDUE	JED & DIANA
THE UNEXPECTED STORM	NEIL & CANDY
THE WEDDING	NEIL & CANDY and the entire Friessen Family

The Friessens:
A New Beginning

THE DEADLINE	ANDY & LAURA
THE PRICE TO LOVE	NEIL & CANDY
A DIFFERENT KIND OF LOVE	BRAD & EMILY
A VOW OF LOVE.	THE ENTIRE
A FRIESSEN FAMILY CHRISTMAS	FRIESSEN FAMILY

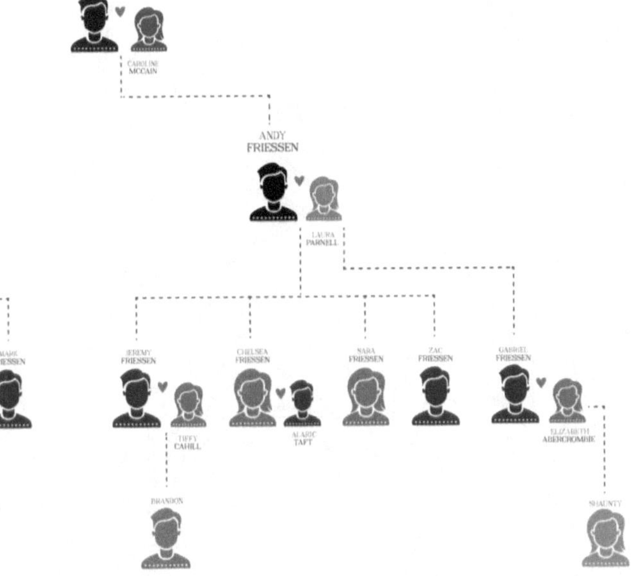

The Friessens

...E ENTIRE FRIESSEN FAMILY	LEAVE THE LIGHT ON — KATY & STEVEN
...DY & LAURA	IN THE MOMENT — BECKY & TOM
...D & DIANA	IN THE FAMILY. *A Friessen Family Christmas* — THE ENTIRE FRIESSEN FAMILY
...IL & CANDY	IN THE SILENCE — CAT & XANDER
...AD & EMILY	IN THE STARS — DANNY & EVIE
...TY & STEVEN	IN THE CHARM — CHRIS & J.D.
...TY & STEVEN	UNEXPECTED CONSEQUENCES — CHRIS & J.D.

The Friessens

IT WAS ALWAYS YOU	KATY & STEVEN
THE FIRST TIME I SAW YOU	GABRIEL & ELIZABETH
WELCOME TO MY ARMS	CHELSEA & ALARIC
WELCOME TO BOSTON	PAIGE & MORGAN
I'LL ALWAYS LOVE YOU	JEREMY
GROUND RULES	JEREMY & TIFFY
A REASON TO BREATHE	TREVOR & JASMINE
YOU ARE MY EVERYTHING	MICHAEL & ANGIE
ANYTHING FOR YOU	
THE HOMECOMING	THE ENTIRE FRIESSEN FAMILY

Chapter One

"So this is what it's come to," Gabriel mumbled under his breath as he waited behind a beefy motorcycle dude with a leather vest, grubby jeans, and tattoos covering one arm, the kind of guy he'd never want to find himself at odds with. That was why, instead of asking him to move, he stood patiently at the back of the corner store, where the community bulletin board was, just so he could pin up his own pitiful request.

The said biker dude was busy taking in the entire board of what looked like dozens of notices, ads, and items for sale, as if reading every printout twice. Gabriel had only another ten minutes before he had to get back to the job site, to his own eye-opening job on a construction crew under a big contractor in the area, doing anything and everything the head supervisor deemed necessary.

The fact was that he was now having to get real and learn skills from the real world since deciding college wasn't for him five years earlier. He was far happier with this hands-on way of learning than with a stuffy classroom, which was another reason he was standing there, staring at the recycled white bond paper on which he'd scribbled his information, looking to find a roommate so he could afford to pay the mortgage and every bill that was piling up for the fixer-upper he'd bought. Although he'd thankfully learned many of the skills to do the work himself, the house had turned into a money pit and had dried up Gabriel's bank account to the red. He was now in overdraft, giving up his source of freedom and opening his house to a stranger.

That was when the biker dude glanced back at Gabriel, his unusual dark eyes pinning him where he was. "Whatcha offering?" He had a raspy voice, the kind that came from smoking too long and too many cigarettes.

Of course, he froze, not knowing what the hell the man was asking. For a second, his brain headed to some pretty lewd places, and he wanted to step back and away, to get the hell out of there, but he gestured to the paper he was holding, or rather gripping, in sweaty hands.

"Uh..." was all he got out before the biker dude reached for the paper and took it from his grip. He grunted as he read the words, his lips moving, and he nodded as if liking what he read. Then he turned and pinned it over the flyer for an upcoming auction for a pickup. Gabriel just stood there with his hands still outstretched, trying to figure out what the fuck had just happened.

"Roommate wanted, your own room and bathroom, shared kitchen..." The man was actually reading it out loud now, and Gabriel had to fight to keep from digging his fingers into his palms as the man flicked his unusual gaze his way. It wasn't so much his face as it was his entire being, his big body, the size of him, and the long gold chain pierced into one ear and hanging to his shoulder. Everything about him screamed that he wasn't someone Gabriel wanted to find himself face to face with in some back alley.

He wanted to back out of there and say it was all a mistake.

"So everything is included in this price, heat, electric, or is anything extra?" The man was still talking to him.

He should say it was taken, ask for the paper back or something, because there was no way he was renting a room in his house to a guy like this. "All included," he said, "but I should add that there's no smoking, parties, or general craziness."

The man made a face and nodded as he glanced back to him. "Yeah, you can't be too careful. All kinds out there. So is it a house or apartment?"

Oh, good God, he was still asking about the place. Gabriel could feel the way his jaw pinched from how tightly he was grinding his teeth. This guy was seriously interested in his listing. This could not be happening. There was no way biker dude was living with him. "House, but then, it has to be the right fit. You know, personalities and all, and cleanliness. There's an expectation that everything will be kept neat and tidy." *Good job!* He crossed his arms and took in the way the guy faced him now and cocked a brow, and his heartbeat kicked up a bit as he wondered whether the guy realized he was referring to him.

"Garage, shed, what about storage options?"

For a second, Gabriel blinked, because the guy hadn't taken the hint. This conversation really was going to a bad place.

"Street parking only, no sheds. It's a nice area, a *family area*." He really emphasized the last point, leaning in a bit, his arms crossed over his chest, hoping the guy got the message so he wouldn't have to spell it out any clearer.

"Perfect!" The man actually reached over and slapped Gabriel on the shoulder, showing his front two teeth with metal caps. Gabriel thought the floor softened beneath his feet as the man reached out and ripped off one of the fifteen slips with his phone number and lifted it in the air. "I'll give this to my sister," he said. "She's looking for a place." He actually held the paper up between his fingers as if to emphasize its importance, and Gabriel made a mental note in that second to make sure he turned her away.

"Hey, Marty," someone called out. "The pop truck is here. I'm going to help unload. Can you watch the front?" The neat and tidy lanky dude Gabriel had spotted behind the front counter strode past, flicking a lock of his long blond hair back. The biker dude shrugged.

Now Gabriel was really looking at the guy and the empty hallway with the sign above that read *Employees only*, which the other guy had just walked down. It had him doing a double take, as he was having trouble understanding. Did the biker guy actually work there?

"Of course," Marty, the biker dude, said and stepped away from the board. Gabriel didn't miss how big he was, at least six foot two, and he had to be close to three hundred pounds, give or take. "Anything else you need?"

He realized Marty was staring down at him. Gabriel was far from a small man, just shy of six feet, with a broad chest and arms and shoulders strong enough to carry some of the heaviest beams on the job site, and he knew well that women appreciated the way he looked. As he stood there, trying to get his brain to kick in and come up with something reasonable and coherent to say, he realized Marty was still waiting patiently for an answer, so Gabriel flicked his hand to the side. "Ah, nope, just needed to put that up. I better get back to work."

He gestured with his thumb behind him and started

backing up, then turned and put one foot in front of the other, getting the hell out that door.

HIS PHONE BUZZED from his back pocket as he stood on the ladder, the support beam on his shoulder. They were one man down today on the crew.

Dwayne, one of the carpenters, sawdust scattered in his dark hair, was hammering the beam in place. "Okay, you can let go now," he said, and Gabriel climbed down, rolling his shoulder and reaching in his pocket.

He pulled out the phone on the third ring. "Gabriel Friessen," he answered, gesturing to Dwayne to give him a minute as the man ran his hand over the pile of two by fours before pulling one out. He turned his back when he heard nothing. "Hello, anyone there?"

"I'm calling about the room you have for rent."

He had to shove his finger in his ear so he could hear as Dwayne started hammering. "Yeah, sorry, there's a lot of background noise here. You're going to have to speak up." He stepped over by the furnace, where the heating guys had just finished.

"The room for rent? You are renting out a room, right?" It was a woman's soft voice, and for a minute, he was about to say it had already been rented, as his first thought was that this must be biker dude's sister. Maybe not, though, considering she didn't sound the crazy type, and nor did he hear anything pointing him in the direction of her being related to biker dude.

"Yeah, a shared house," he said. "It's a bedroom that comes with your own bathroom." He walked across the room into where the kitchen would be, stepping over the plywood floors, seeing that the room had been taken back to the studs. There was silence again. "Hello, are you still there?"

"Is the bedroom furnished?"

He wondered for a second whether she'd hang up when he told her he had a sofa only and hadn't bothered to buy anything else.

"No, you'll have to bring your own bed. It's just a room. Look, if you'd like to see it, we can meet, but I'll stress that I have others seeing it, so bring references, and…" *And what?* he thought. These "others" hadn't yet called.

"So you have a lot of people coming to see it?" She had such a soft voice.

"I'll be showing it tonight." *To hopefully more than one person.*

"And everything is included in the price of four hundred?"

"Everything." He nodded to Dwayne, who called out to him. "Come by around seven," he said and rattled off his address, making a quick mental note to clean up the dirty dishes, laundry, and garbage he had lying around.

His hair was damp, and he was wearing his only clean pair of jeans, a faded pair with a tear in the thigh, as he tied up the black garbage bag and then ran his hand over the teal granite of his island counter in the kitchen. It was one of the best rooms in the house since he'd renovated and rebuilt it, opening it up to the living and dining room to make it open. The white cabinets with glass fronts gave it a high-end look, as did the gas stove and pot filler. The new stainless-steel appliances were the icing on the cake and one of the many reasons he needed to rent out a piece of this house. The reno had been expensive, especially given all the problems he'd discovered behind the walls on demolition.

He glanced at the clock, then down at his phone on the counter, seeing he still had no calls. Not one call for the room other than the lady coming now. What the hell? He'd expected to have his phone blowing up with messages, considering the price and the lack of places to rent. For his sake, he hoped biker dude wasn't showing up with the lady. Even better, he hoped the lady coming now was no relation. If she was his sister, he'd show her around, take her references, and walk her the hell out of there.

He picked up the black garbage bag. It was almost seven, judging by the large centerpiece clock on the otherwise bare living room wall, and he ran his hand over his bare chest. Yeah, he still needed to find a shirt, a clean one, which he'd do right after he tucked the garbage in the can outside. He pulled open the front door and stopped, taking in the long dark hair and slim curves of a gorgeous woman. She was holding the hand of what seemed to be a little girl of three or four, maybe.

"Uh, hi," he said, running his hand over his bare chest again and seeing that her eyes went straight there and then up. Her big bold eyes were the color of toffee, and she didn't smile. Her gaze didn't linger on him at all, either.

"I called about the room to rent," she said. "My name is Elizabeth Abercrombie." She actually held out her hand. He took in the garbage he was holding and switched it to his other hand before giving his free one a quick wipe on his jeans and checking it to make sure it was clean. He took her slender hand in his, surprised by the firm handshake.

"Gabriel Friessen," he said, still holding her hand as he glanced down at the little girl again. She was looking up at him with the same eyes and a shoulder-length mop of out-of-control curls.

Elizabeth pulled her hand away, and he glanced over her head to the street, seeing only his faded blue pickup out front before dragging his gaze back to the attractive woman, who still wasn't smiling.

"I didn't hear a car," he said as she pulled her hand away.

"We took the bus," she said. He noticed the big purse over her shoulder, light tan and black. She had no rings on her fingers.

"I just need to dump this in the trash can," he explained and stepped outside onto the front porch, taking in her cutoffs and loose white shirt. Gorgeous legs, too.

She pointed at the garbage bag in his hand, maybe because he was staring a few seconds too long. "You said you were going to put that in the garbage," she said as if he needed a reminder.

"Right." He strode barefoot down the steps, knowing he was staring and acting like…well, like a man who'd lost his reasoning. She was nothing like what he'd been expecting. She definitely couldn't be related to the biker dude, because she was gorgeous, a sweet girl-next-door package. He felt a moment of relief as he pulled open the garbage can by the front gate and dumped the bag in.

"This is a very nice porch," she said. "You don't see many houses anymore with these old-fashioned columns. It's nice, and it's great that this house is close to the bus stop." She was looking at the freshly painted white columns, the brand-new rail, and the finished deck, which had one red and white lawn chair, the only outdoor furnishing he could afford.

Then she was staring at him, and it took him a second before he realized he was doing it again, staring as if he'd never seen a sexy woman before. She seemed to radiate something that he didn't want to turn away from. "Ah, yeah, the house." He gestured to the door, taking in the little girl. He thought it was a girl, or maybe a boy? She wore a striped T-shirt and blue shorts, with white sneakers on her feet. *Quiet thing.*

"So you're looking for a place to rent, just you?" he asked as he strode up the steps, still barefoot, then stopped before her and looked down. He saw her jaw firm as she glanced over to the kid beside her. When he took her in again, he didn't miss the raised brow. She had caught his meaning.

"This is Shaunty, my daughter. The room is for us—*just us*," she added. "But it's more important that it's clean and reasonable and quiet." She spoke matter of factly, and she looked him square in the eye, not lingering on his chest at all. Her gaze told him she wasn't buying anything. He didn't know why he found it amusing.

"Right, well, come in. I'll show you around." He pulled open the door and gestured, so she went in first and said something to the little girl, who took off her shoes. Elizabeth then slipped off her sandals and stepped into the house, which opened into the living room. It had wood floors, bold gray walls, a flat-screen TV, and a sofa opposite. That was it. "Sorry," he said. "I just finished renovating and haven't had a chance to buy furniture yet."

The truth was that he didn't have a dime to spare to buy anything else.

"This is nice," she said as she walked in, and he watched her taking in the open-concept kitchen before glancing over to the empty dining room with double doors that went out back to a deck. She was walking into the kitchen, running her hand over the countertop, and taking in the appliances, the double-wide fridge, the dishwasher, the gas range. He couldn't help noticing the way she moved, and her daughter stayed right beside her, so well behaved.

"Uh, we'd share the fridge," he said. "I'd clear you some shelves to keep your food."

What was he doing? He didn't know a thing about her, and then there was her kid.

She didn't seem surprised, as she inclined her head. "So who else lives here?" At least she was asking the right questions.

"Just me."

She nodded. "Can I see where the bedroom is, the bathroom?"

He lifted his hand, the hand that had been crossed over his chest. "Of course, this way." He led her across the living room and down a short hall to the first room on the right. The door was open, and he flicked on the light, taking in the small room with its cream walls and white trim.

"This is the room," he said. "There's a small closet with shelves, so you'd be sharing. There's another bedroom next door, but it's stuffed with all my junk, so I won't be renting it out."

He looked down at her, seeing the top of her dark hair. It was deep and rich. The color shimmered, and her hair fell in soft waves to midback. She was so tiny, maybe five two, three tops. Then he took in the little girl, who watched him in a way that made him positive she knew he was checking out her mom before she stated, "Me and Mom sleep together," as if that was everything.

He was surprised she was still watching him. Shaunty…an unusual name. Elizabeth ruffled the little girl's hair and tossed her an easy smile before taking her hand in a protective motherly grip. When she looked up at him, the smile disappeared. "So it doesn't come furnished?" she asked, and for a minute he thought he saw something hopeful in her face.

"No, sorry. As I said on the phone, it doesn't. That's not a problem, is it?"

She just firmed her lips, pink full lips, and then shook her head. "Of course not," she replied, and she said nothing else as she stood in the bedroom, holding her little girl's hand, waiting for him to do what?

He stepped out of the bedroom. "Bathroom is across

the hall, which would be yours. I have my own in the master suite." His own, he thought, with a soaker tub and a steam shower, another feature he hadn't been about to cut back on. He opened the door and flicked on the light. "Bath and shower combo, storage under the sink."

"Oh, Mom, look, two sinks!" Shaunty said. "And two mirrors!"

"I just need to pick up a shower curtain, but this would be yours," Gabriel said.

"Very nice, thank you," Elizabeth said. "And there's laundry?"

He wondered what accent he was picking up in her voice. It was soft, just a hint of something that said she was from a little further south, maybe.

"At the back door, other side of the kitchen." He started down the hall, and she fell in beside him. The little girl, he noticed, was curious about him, from the glances she kept tossing his way.

"So are you from around here?" he said. "Tell me about yourself." He gestured toward her as they walked through the kitchen to the laundry area at the back door, where the laundry basket was on top of the front-loading dryer. He spotted an unfolded clean white shirt and reached for it, finally pulling it on.

"Not much to say about me," Elizabeth said. "I've been here in Columbia Falls for close to ten years. Other than that, I'm hardworking. It's just me and Shaunty. I work part time now at the Moto Auto parts shop, at the front counter. My hours were just cut, though, from full time to half time, leaving me with just four three-hour shifts a week. I'm looking for a different job with more hours, but there's not a lot available right now, which is why I need the room only. It's all I can afford. Just so we're being up front here, I'm single. Was in a relationship, and it didn't end well, and I'm not looking to get into anything anytime soon. Shaunty is four, goes to preschool during the day and daycare when I'm working. We're quiet and expect the same."

She crossed her arms, and he couldn't help noticing her amazing figure again. She still hadn't smiled. Man, she appeared so serious, and he didn't miss her demand.

"Of course, it goes both ways, mutual respect and compatibility," he said. Now, why would he add that? "I mean, not compatible in the relationship kind of way, but yeah, it kind of is, like living together, sharing a roof…" He took in the little girl looking up at him. Maybe she was waiting for him to pull out the foot he'd jammed in his mouth.

"What else do you need to know?" she asked. "Because I'd like to take it. It's clean, nice, reasonable." She lifted her fingers and glanced down to her daughter as if they both agreed, and they both nodded. "And close to the bus stop."

"And don't forget the park, Mom," Shaunty said. She was so cute, the way she talked.

"Right, how could I forget? The park is up the street." She actually winked at her daughter.

Gabriel knew he needed to ask her more questions, more anything, but when he opened his mouth, all that came out was, "Well, great. So when do you want to move in?"

Chapter Three

"Don't look at him, don't smile. Whatever you do, just get those thoughts out of your head," Elizabeth said under her breath as she stood with a big apple box just outside the gate of her new home.

Damn, she was still rattled after meeting Gabriel Friessen, with his unmistakable sexy eyes that made her breath catch in her lungs, and that had prompted the pep talk and reminder that nothing good ever came from tall, dark, and handsome. So she juggled the box and reached around to unlatch the gate.

"Oh, let me get that for you, sugar," her mother said, unlatching the gate for Elizabeth. Chloe had brown hair and a short cut that resembled a football. Her ginormous earrings, a mix of brass and silver, dangled to her shoulders.

"Mom, you know dressing up for moving day kind of defeats the purpose of helping me move," Elizabeth said.

Her mom had a blue handbag that matched her ridiculous outfit looped over her arm. She wore a long, flowing loose sundress of mixed blues that stopped at mid-calf, with three-inch wedge heels and the same plastered-on makeup she wore every day. Elizabeth had seen her mom without makeup only once, and it had taken her a minute to get her brain to realize that the woman was in fact her mother.

"Nonsense," Chloe said. "You should always put your best foot forward and look your very best every time you step out the door. I'm even opening the gate for you, since you can't do that yourself because your hands are full… Frank, are you bringing those bags up? Come on, hurry up now," her mom called out over her shoulder to her dad.

Frank was a big man, tall, with deep eyes, and he always shopped in the extra-large section. He lifted his hand and, she was pretty sure, grunted. At the same time, her mom was still talking, or nagging, about something as she walked away. Elizabeth, like her dad, had stopped listening after the first few words. Chloe seemed to go on and on forever.

She hoofed it up the five wide stairs to the gorgeous three-bedroom house, which had a sweet homey feel the likes of which she'd never experienced, and to boot, it was first class, the kind of home she'd dreamed of having. She still couldn't believe she'd told Gabriel the unfurnished room wasn't a problem, though. Well, she'd been through worse, so having to camp out on a blowup mattress and use boxes to store their clothes would be a small inconvenience, considering she now had a place for her and Shaunty.

She pulled the keys to the front door from the pocket of her faded blue jeans, the keys Gabriel had given her yesterday, but the front door opened before she could use them. There stood mister tall, dark, and handsome himself, this time appearing somewhat decent, wearing a faded pair of jeans, a red T-shirt, and a smile that only had her frowning.

"Oh, hi, I didn't think you'd be here," she stated. Actually, for a minute, she wondered if she'd snarled it. It was what she had hoped, even though the opposite was true, if she was being honest.

"It's Saturday, my day off. Thought I told you I'd be around." He stepped out the door, leaving it open, angling his head to the side and looking around her as he took in her parents. She could still hear her mom talking. Well, words were coming out of her mouth, but she wasn't listening to any of it.

"My parents." She gestured toward them, juggling the box, and almost dropped it.

"Let me." His hand covered hers, and he took the box from her before she could say anything. She pulled her hand back from the touch, which shot fire through her. There was no way in hell she was going to let herself feel that, so she fisted her hand and forced a smile to her face.

"You know what? I can carry my own boxes." She forced the words out and took in the moment he registered what she'd said. He actually handed her back the box and stepped away, lifting his hands in the air. Of course, now she felt like a first-class bitch, but boundaries were imperative, and the last thing she ever planned on happening was getting sucked into another pair of dreamy eyes, a killer smile, and a rugged body she could stare at all day. No way. Been there, done that.

"After you…" he started just as the voices behind them grew louder. Her mom was walking up the sidewalk carrying nothing other than her handbag, whereas her dad was carrying two big suitcases. Her mom went on and on about something she didn't have a clue about.

"Mom, Dad, this is Gabriel," she called out as she stepped into the house and glanced at the clean floors and her shoes. "Is it okay if we leave our shoes on?" she said as her dad nodded and her mom shook Gabriel's hand.

"Oh, so nice to meet you," Chloe said. "Gabriel, is it? Tell me, what is your family name? Who are your people, and where are you from?"

Elizabeth took in what she could only assume was a thrown expression on Gabriel's face. Yup, that was exactly what her mom was famous for.

He darted a glance back to her and shrugged. "Ah… don't worry about your shoes."

She kept walking, hearing him say something to her mom, who she knew would be dogging him with questions, a lot of questions. Then she'd report back to Elizabeth and everyone else exactly what she'd learned.

She stepped into her bedroom, her and Shaunty's, and instantly had to take a breath, a deep breath, as she felt a huge chunk of the tension she'd been carrying fall away. She rested the box of her photos and personal junk on the floor in the corner and took in the closed blinds. The room was stuffy and warm. She pulled the blinds up and took in the window, the latch, but when she flicked it open and pulled, nothing happened. She flicked the latch the other way, and again nothing budged.

"What are you doing, Lizzy?" her dad asked. She could hear him huffing as if he'd run up the street, but she knew it was all that fried food, bags of chips and everything else, that he was always eating.

"Trying to open this window, but it's stuck or something…" She pulled again, yanked with both hands.

"Ah, let me open it. You see, you just need to put muscle into it, is all." Her dad put down the big orange suitcases she'd had forever. The empty room had something of an echo.

She stepped away and lifted her hand. "Fine, you see if

you can open it, and I'll go get the rest of my things." Elizabeth stepped out of the bedroom and started to the front door, hearing her dad grunting as he yanked and yanked, then started cursing at the window, something else he did with anything that wasn't working for him.

"So you have how many brothers and sisters, and where do they live?" Her mom had Gabriel in the kitchen, where she was opening up the fridge and still peppering him with questions. For the most part, Gabriel seemed to be holding up okay.

"Hey, great, you got a second, Elizabeth?" He turned his head so fast from her mom, and his expression said everything.

"Sure." She started over to the kitchen.

"Lizzy, have you seen in here, this fridge? There's no food in here. He has no real food. Where are the pickles, ketchup, sour cream, Cheez Whiz? It's just greens, and what's this here…" Her mom was actually pulling things out of the fridge and setting them on the counter as she held up a jar. "Kim…chi? What is this stuff? Oh, look, there's even tofu and MCT oil." Her mom was really going to town.

"That's kimchi. I eat a really clean diet," he stated.

"Well, I've never heard of such a thing. Can't taste any good." Of course, she was still going on about the food.

"Mom, Mom…" Elizabeth actually stepped forward and tapped the counter with her hand to get her mom's attention.

"What, baby?" The way she said it as she turned around, holding a bag of bean sprouts, she sounded as if she was interrupting her.

"Put the food back," Elizabeth said and gestured with her finger, then flicked her hand again and again to the fridge. "Seriously, Mom, put it back and stop it already. That food belongs to Gabriel."

"I don't know how you call this food. Where are the Hungry-Man TV dinners in your freezer, the Tater Tots…" Her mom was still talking as she turned around and put the lettuce, the greens, the jars back in the fridge.

Gabriel was now walking around the island, his eyes glued to her. "Can I talk to you a second, outside?"

"Of course," she said. She didn't realize he was bare-footed until he walked to the open front door. She could hear her dad from the bedroom.

"Come on, you motherfucker, open!" he said, followed by an *oomph* sound.

Gabriel turned his sharp gaze her way and then back down the hall to where her dad was still cursing and yelling.

She gestured helplessly. "Window's stuck. Dad's trying to open it."

His eyes widened. "Ah!" He hurried down the hall to her bedroom. "Hey, just hold up and don't pull—"

She heard what sounded like breaking glass. "Oh, shit, no!" she muttered and jogged to the room to find a hole where her window should be. The blinds were hanging to one side, and one of the panes of glass was shattered on the floor.

Chapter Four

It really was on him, Gabriel thought. He should have said something about the window. It had a defective latch that opened only when he slid the lock to the center. It was one of the few things he was planning on talking to Elizabeth about, but then her dad, a big lug of a guy, had taken care of the problem in another way. Now he was staring at broken glass, a hole he'd need to fix, and the back-and-forth arguing from Frank and Chloe, Elizabeth's odd and eccentric nosy parents.

"I am so sorry," Elizabeth said, and he took in her hand pressed flat to her chest, the sweetheart neckline of her faded blue tank showing a hint of cleavage.

"It's fine," he said, though it wasn't, really. Now he'd have to put out for a new window, and windows weren't cheap.

"No, it's not fine. I'll pay for it, of course, and clean it up." She was already kneeling down on the floor, about to pick up the glass.

"No, Elizabeth, I'll get a broom and sweep it up—"

Chloe interrupted. "Just tell me where your broom is.

Frank here will sweep it up," she said, and he noted the hint of a southern accent as she stepped in and gestured to the mess.

"It's in the laundry room. Just let me grab the garbage can to dump all this in."

Gabriel stepped out of the room, taking in his bare feet, and he stopped at the open front door, hearing the voices of Elizabeth and her parents. He shoved his feet into his sneakers and went into the laundry room to grab the broom and dust pan before stopping again at the front door and spotting one of the empty plastic cans by the gate. He leaned the broom against the wall and went outside, grabbed the plastic can, and walked back in the house with it, then hoofed it down the hall and saw all three pair of eyes turn to him.

"Oh, we'll take that from you," Chloe said. "Frank, you can clean this mess up…" The broom was taken from his hand, the garbage can too, and Elizabeth was rolling her eyes and walking his way.

"You got a second?" she said as she stepped out of the room and into the hall. "Again, I am so sorry about the window. My dad tries to help, but…" She gestured helplessly.

"No, it's no biggie. I'll get another window in." *And be a few hundred more bucks in the hole,* he thought. "But we should square up a few other things. I haven't seen your little girl, Shaunty?"

She smiled as she stepped outside onto the front porch. She had an incredible smile. "She's with my sister, Ruby. She said she's taking her to the park, but that's more a ruse to take her to the shopping mall, where she's likely going to come home with a few too many useless toys, outfits she can't wear, and things she doesn't need."

Ah, so there was a sister too. Her mother was intrusive,

all right. No, he was still feeling as if he'd been nipped in the ass by a passing tornado. "Anyway, you have the keys, and the rent…" he started.

She reached into her back pocket and pulled out a wad of bills. "As promised, four hundred dollars." She handed him the cash. "It's all there, but feel free to count it," she added.

For a second, he wondered whether she was insinuating something, from the way she said it, but then he couldn't tell for sure. "No, no, of course not." He tucked the cash in his pocket. "Hey, I thought maybe we could sit down after and talk. Maybe you have questions…" He let it hang, taking in the way she stared back at him as if she wasn't impressed. Okay, so no chitchat right now. "Or maybe I can help you bring in furniture, the bed, dresser, anything else you have."

Why was he babbling? She opened her mouth as if to say something and instead just pulled in a breath before closing her mouth and squinting, then glancing out and down the street.

"No furniture," she said. "Just an air mattress and some blankets to bring in, and then I'd say we're set." She started down the steps and out the open gate, not waiting for him to say anything. She stopped at an older-model Lincoln that had a huge open trunk. This was it, an air mattress for her and her little girl?

Then he heard a really loud motorcycle and turned with Elizabeth to see a bike coming toward them, one of those long Harleys. It pulled up in front of his truck and stopped. *Ah, shit, biker dude.* On the back was a kid wearing a helmet.

"Marty, what the hell are you doing putting Shaunty on your bike? I told you before I don't want her riding on it. Come on, hop down, honey."

He watched as Elizabeth lifted Shaunty off the bike just as the kid unfastened the too-big helmet. Marty then turned off the engine, which rumbled with an awful racket. He had to fight the urge to look over his shoulder to see if any of the neighbors had stepped out of their houses, maybe to see who it was who would be pulling into a neighborhood that was all families, middle class, an ultra-conservative lot who he figured were all in bed by nine.

"Ruby got called into work," Marty said, "and you know how she can never say no to a shift for extra cash, so she called me and I swooped on down and picked up my niece." He lifted off his black helmet and stepped off the bike the way guys do, lifting his leg over the seat and resting the helmet on it as he winked at the little girl, who actually winked back.

"No, the problem is that Ruby spends money faster than she can make it on the slots. She's never learned to prioritize anything or follow through on a promise."

Gabriel picked up the edge in Elizabeth's voice and figured it would be wise to keep his mouth shut, considering he was still stuck on the fact that biker dude was there. At the same time, he was at a loss as to how something like this could happen. How could Elizabeth in any way be related to this unnerving man, who could be affiliated with some really bad people? It was the kind of thing he didn't want around him.

Marty turned his piercing hard gaze on Gabriel before sticking out his hand as he walked over to him. "See you met my sister, and thanks for renting her a room. She said it's real sweet looking."

Gabriel was used to strong grips, but the way this guy squeezed his hand and then pulled him into him, he bounced off his chest.

Marty slapped his back. "Don't mess with my sister,"

he said in a low voice in Gabriel's ear before he could step back.

What the hell was he supposed to say to that? He took in Elizabeth squatting down before the little girl, ignoring both of them, and he couldn't figure out how she fit with Marty and the odd couple inside his house. *His house!*

Marty slapped his hands together. The fat in his bare arms wobbled over the muscle he had felt from that grip. "Well, come on, show me around," he said. "I want to see these new digs of yours."

Gabriel just stood there and watched as Marty strode up to his house, and he was left standing with Elizabeth and her little girl.

Elizabeth made a face and shrugged. "That's my brother, Marty. I'm wondering by your face if you're now regretting renting a room to us."

He didn't know what to say as he looked down at Shaunty, who was holding her mother's hand, quiet, polite, her hair sticking up everywhere. Elizabeth was standing there, looking gorgeous, and she still didn't fit the mold of this crazy family that seemed to have taken over his house.

"Of course not. I'll get this." He lifted out the blankets before Elizabeth stepped over to the trunk and rested her hand on his arm.

"Just in case I didn't say it, Gabriel, thank you." She said it so humbly before pulling her hand away, looking down to Shaunty, and walking away with her, carrying a bag stuffed with clothes and talking to her daughter as if he didn't even exist.

Chapter Five

"Take my bed."

That had been what he'd said to her after her family had left and she'd been sitting on the floor of her room, blowing up the double mattress that had been leaking from a tiny hole in the side. By the time he had called the glass company to order a new window, they had been closed, and they would be until Monday. With a sheet of plywood over where the window should be, she considered the offer only once before she glanced to her daughter and said yes.

Now here she was in the grocery store two blocks away, and Gabriel was where? Outside in the parking lot, because he was determined to be a gentleman and drive her to the store even though she had two feet and could walk. "So what are we buying?" her daughter asked as they walked along the back of the store.

Elizabeth was pushing a cart through the bakery and dairy aisle. "Food until next week, and we're going to need to be really frugal."

Shaunty walked along beside the cart and nodded as if

that made sense, then looked up to her, her expression priceless. "What does frugal mean?"

She fought the urge to laugh. "It means we can't spend much, so think cheap. We buy what's marked down." Next Friday she would get another check for her part-time hours, and then she could put aside enough for rent and buy more food. Great way to live, paycheck to paycheck.

"So like macaroni and cheese," her daughter added, sounding more responsible than most adults. She had to pinch herself for being so lucky to have such a great kid. She nodded as she took in her gorgeous, beautiful, smart-as-a-whip daughter, thankful the only thing she'd gotten from her useless, idiot father was his hair.

"Exactly, so we'll stick to everything that's cheap and on sale, like macaroni, bread, peanut butter, and milk." They would need to skip the eggs, buy the cheapest cuts of meat on sale, and prioritize. Her daughter had scored on the macaroni: The no-name brand was marked down. They found a bag of carrots, too, and she loaded up the cart with as much as she could, adding up in her head as she went.

Elizabeth unloaded the cart at the cash register and watched as the cashier rang it up, hoping she'd done the math correctly.

"Hey there, you're almost done." She jumped and turned when Gabriel appeared beside her. He pulled off his sunglasses and rested them atop his head in his short, messy dark hair. It too was sexy as all hell.

"Yeah, I'm, uh…"

"That will be $68.25," the cashier said, and her heart sank. She'd miscounted, having only fifty-two dollars and twelve cents. She touched her head, lifting her purse on the counter, feeling her daughter beside her. The customers behind them were already unloading their groceries.

She leaned in. "Sorry, I'm short. I'll have to put some things back…" She was flustered as she scanned the groceries, trying to quickly figure out what to take out. "Can you take off the bag of apples, and…" She took in the carrots, the milk, bread, peanut butter, tuna, mayonnaise. "The mayonnaise, too."

The cashier gave her an annoyed glance, and she could feel her face burn in embarrassment as she heard the woman waiting behind her let out a huff of annoyance.

"Don't put it back. Hey, how much do you need?" Gabriel stepped closer to her, and she wished he hadn't. In fact, it would be better if he'd just turn and leave and let her deal with this as quickly and with as much dignity as she could.

"No, that's fine, really. I just need to take out a few things I don't really need…"

He was pulling out his wallet, and the cashier was leveling a hard glance her way that said, *Stop wasting my time.* She shoved her hand in her purse and pulled out her wallet. "Fine, about fourteen dollars and…" She fumbled, feeling sweat running down her back, and her hand was shaking as she pulled out the bills.

Gabriel handed his debit card to the cashier. "Just put it on here," he said, and she lifted her hand to gesture something, but she could feel the other shoppers listening in on everything.

"You don't have to do this," she whispered to Gabriel and pulled out all her bills, then dumped her coins out into her hand as he punched his number into the debit machine. The cashier bagged up the groceries, and he shoved his card back in his wallet. She went to hand him the cash and her handful of coins, but he just stared at her hand, then looked up to her.

He shook his head before lifting her two bags of groceries and said, "It's fine. We'll square it up later."

She was forced to shove the money back in her wallet, grab Shaunty's hand, and hurry to follow Gabriel and his long strides out of the store. She was humiliated and furious at Gabriel at the same time.

"Seriously, you didn't need to do that. I'll pay you back for all of it, but you shouldn't have done it," she said as she followed him out to his pickup, and she didn't miss the cut of his biceps, his strong forearms in his simple T-shirt, and the way he seemed to easily carry the bags as if they were nothing. "I've got fifty-two dollars and would have preferred to just put something back. I don't like owing anyone."

He stopped at his pickup and rested the bags in the back of the flatbed, then rested his forearms on the edge. He glanced over to her as he settled his sunglasses back on, and she didn't miss the odd look in his face as if he couldn't figure out what to say.

"How about a 'Thank you, Gabriel'? Just a simple thank-you. Seriously, I have never met a woman who has so many walls up and makes things so much harder than they need to be. It's not a big deal. It's food, and you have a daughter to feed. You can pay me back." Then he pulled open the driver's door, and she looked down to her daughter, who was standing there so quietly, staring up at her as if she agreed with everything Gabriel had said.

"It's okay, Mom. He's nice, you can pay him back." She sounded so reasonable, but she had no idea of the cost of becoming beholden to anyone. She just hoped her daughter never had to figure that out.

"Okay, climb in," she said as she pulled open the passenger side, and her daughter scooted into the middle of the pickup. Gabriel was already behind the wheel and was reaching around to fasten Shaunty's seat belt.

"Lizzie!"

She heard the deep voice shout out, and she jerked her head back just as she was about to slip into the truck.

"Oh, shit," she said as she stared at MM, a.k.a. Mac Murrin, digging into each step and coming right for her from across the parking lot. He had thick kinky dark hair, and he was a big dude with killer abs, a broad chest, and strong arms that pumped double his body weight. It was his amazing physique that she'd totally fallen for, but it had been his dimpled grin and icy blue eyes that had sunk her. He was wearing a wrinkled tank and worn blue jeans, with a chain hanging from his pocket attached to a pocket watch, and his face had a five o'clock shadow.

"Hey, everything okay?" Gabriel asked, and she glanced into the truck and saw her daughter unfasten her belt, look up, and then slide over to the edge before bolting out of the truck.

"Daddy!" she said as she raced over to MM, who lifted her with a toss before catching her and then swinging her around like an airplane in the busy mall lot.

"Are you following me?" Elizabeth said. That would be just like him. She watched as he slung Shaunty over his shoulder as if she were a sack of potatoes.

"Hell, no," he said. "Just drove into the parking lot and couldn't believe I saw you with some slick-looking dude and my daughter. What the hell, Lizzie? You moving on on me? I went to the Grove, and they said you moved out. I drove around all night looking for you. You get your ass back in my car and out of this truck. You ain't going anywhere until I decide I'm done with you, you cold-hearted bitch."

She could feel eyes on her from the supermarket.

People were staring. She heard the slam of the truck door and knew that Gabriel had stepped out, and that was a problem, because MM was unpredictable.

"Well, that's the thing, MM. I told you before, every time you show up at a place of mine, that we're done. We're over. No more sleeping outside the door to my place, no more following me around, no more showing up at my work, so kindly put Shaunty down, and we're going to be on our way." She was afraid to look over to Gabriel, because she feared what she'd see there.

"You sleeping with my girlfriend?" MM said. "Well, I ought to teach you a lesson, you fucking little pissant..." He put down Shaunty, who ran over to Elizabeth. Oh, shit, this wasn't good.

"Get in the truck, honey," she said. MM was digging into each step, heading right for Gabriel, his fists ready and his expression that of the idiot she'd left, whose entire reasoning centered around his fists. "MM, don't you dare!" she called out.

He was around the truck, in Gabriel's face, and Gabriel wore the same *What the fuck?* look everyone did when they first encountered MM.

"Are you crazy?" Gabriel just stood there, and Elizabeth grabbed MM's arm before he could swing and bust Gabriel's face.

Next thing she knew, she was flying into the blue car parked next to them. "Ugh!" she grunted out as she slid down the car to the ground, wondering for a second whether anything was broken. She was dizzy and thought she saw stars.

"Oh my God, Lizzie, are you okay? I'm so sorry, baby," MM said. He was on the ground now, kneeling down.

She was on all fours, trying to catch her breath from the ache in her side and her shoulder where she'd slammed into the car. MM's hands were on her, and she slid around on her ass and sat there, leaning against some stranger's car. She couldn't seem to get rid of the crazy idiot in front of her. Then there was Gabriel, who was leaning into the truck and saying something to her daughter. When he stood up, she saw he had his cell phone to his ear.

She wanted to weep as she sat there, feeling she was hitting rock bottom, all because MM wouldn't take the hint or hear that they were done. She knew this was it, and she'd once again have to move to get away from this idiot.

Chapter Six

"Like, what the fuck?" Gabriel muttered. This was at least the tenth time he'd said it under his breath as he took in the flashing lights of the cops, whom he'd called because there was no way he was taking on a crazed idiot who was hell bent on killing him. Elizabeth's crazy ex—who, as he now had figured out, was also Shaunty's father—was still carrying on, yelling and screaming obscenities toward him in between pleas for Elizabeth to take him back, even though he was cuffed and being wrestled by two deputies into the back of a cop car. Gabriel couldn't make any sense of it. Even after the cops shut the door, the man was still yelling, and Gabriel was pretty sure all manner of threats were being directed at him.

This was absolutely insane.

"I'm fine, really, it's okay," he heard Elizabeth say to her daughter, who was sitting on the edge of the driver's seat now, leaning out the open door of the truck. Elizabeth was standing in front of her. Gabriel had expected the kid to be crying, freaking out, but she wasn't. Instead, he heard her ask again if her mom was okay. She was only four!

The driver of the blue car Elizabeth had slammed into had returned, and thankfully there was no dent in the side from how hard she'd been thrown against it. The driver had backed out and left after asking only a question or two, leaving the spot empty. Gabriel now had room to walk back and forth as he took in the scene, gave his statement, and finally rested his arm over the back of the truck.

He ran his other hand over his head, watching Elizabeth and seeing the moment she made a face and touched her side. Yeah, she was hurt. He should go to her, say something, but what?

One of the deputies walked around Gabriel and over to Elizabeth, wearing a tan shirt and mirrored shades. "Okay, so again, about what happened, did he hit you or didn't he? To hold him on assault charges…"

"He didn't hit me," she said, and the deputy stepped back from the truck and appeared to take in Shaunty's wide eyes as she looked between him and her mom, not saying a word. "He was going to hit Gabriel. I just got in the way and tried to stop him, grabbed his arm. Big mistake. Got tossed into the car. But that was an accident, as much as I'd like to say otherwise."

Gabriel shook his head and had to press his lips together, because he wanted to say a few things to Elizabeth. When he glanced over, he didn't miss the way she was watching him and holding her arm.

"If he'd hit me or intentionally thrown me into the car, I'd say it," she said. "But he didn't, and I'm not about to lie. He won't leave me alone, though. Could you do something about that? Because that's what I'd really like."

The crazy guy was still staring daggers Gabriel's way, tucked in the back of the cop car, and he was so big that he seemed to take up much of the back seat.

"You got a restraining order?"

She didn't say anything, just stared at the cop, who had his hands on his hips. Then she slowly shook her head. "No, because when I went to a free consultation with a notary, he said that unless I felt my life was in danger, a restraining order would be costly and not worth the nuisance he's being," she added dryly and with a hint of sarcasm, he thought.

"Well, then all we can do is charge him with disorderly conduct, which means he'll likely be slapped with only a hundred-dollar fine. There's nothing else I can do." The dark-haired cop was still wearing his shades, and Gabriel noted the badge pinned to his shirt and the gun holstered to his belt as he turned to face him. "Is there anything else?"

Gabriel pushed away from the truck and looked around the cop to Elizabeth, who looked like a kicked puppy, though he knew she was doing her best to hide her disappointment. "I guess not. You're taking him to jail, though, right?"

The cop actually stepped around him and rested his hand on his shoulder. "We are. He'll go before a judge and be out in the morning. My advice, hire a lawyer, get something with some teeth in it, and then, if there's a next time, maybe then we can do something."

Gabriel watched as the cop walked to the car, climbed in, and drove away, Elizabeth's crazy ex in tow. Then he took in Elizabeth wincing as she helped Shaunty down.

"What are you doing?" he said.

She flicked up those amber eyes, which weren't shining quite as bright now. "Helping my daughter down so we can go."

For a second, he wasn't sure what she meant. "Well, yeah, we should go, so you kind of both need to get back in the truck."

She didn't move. She just stared at him and blinked. "You mean you still want us to come with you…?" She let her words fall away, and he understood what she was saying.

"You rented a room, I drove you to the store for food, and now you think I'm going to kick you out?" Did she really think he was some kind of scumbag? What did she think he would say? *Geez, your crazy ex is a handful and totally insane, so now I'm going to kick you to the curb.* He didn't say that, though, because he saw it in the way she worked her mouth, trying to figure out what to say.

"Well, I wouldn't have blamed you if you did. You didn't sign on for this craziness. So you're telling me it's fine, that we're…" She gestured and then glanced down to her little girl, who was watching Gabriel as if she expected…what? He didn't have a clue. She was the most intriguing, smart little kid he'd ever met.

"You know what? I'm starving," he said. "You two have to be as well. Let's go home, make dinner."

Shaunty climbed back in the truck, and when Elizabeth started around him, he couldn't help but rest his hand on her arm, feeling how tight she was.

"I never asked if you were okay," he said.

She didn't look at him for a second, but when she did, she just shrugged and then stared at his hand until he let it fall away. "I'm fine," she said. "Been through worse. I'm tough, and it would take a lot more than that to hurt me."

He didn't miss the smile that touched her lips as she walked around him to the passenger side of the truck and climbed in, but he was damn sure she was hurting a lot more than she was saying.

She was putting on a brave front in a situation where anyone else would have shed a few tears and been not quite as together, but here she was now, sitting beside her daughter in the cab of his truck, facing forward with what seemed like a ten-inch-thick wall of armor keeping everyone from getting too close.

As he stared out in the distance to the cop car that was long gone, he realized that if the roles were reversed, he'd likely be a little prickly too.

Chapter Seven

Gabriel was chopping greens and washing lettuce while a piece of wild salmon was grilling in the oven, and Elizabeth was standing by the gas stove, waiting for the water to boil so she could pour in the macaroni. She'd already tucked away the few dry goods she'd bought —or, rather, the ones Gabriel had paid for—in a cupboard and put the milk, cheese, ground beef, and carrots in the fridge. At least now they could have tuna sandwiches with mayo, although lettuce was out. Tomorrow she'd figure out something to make with the ground beef, and then hopefully a way to stretch it for the week.

"You sure you don't want some salad, too? I have extra," Gabriel said as she watched him mixing olive oil and apple cider vinegar in a jar with some fresh herbs he'd just finished chopping.

"No, macaroni is fine," she said, even though his dinner seemed far more appealing. They'd have sliced carrots, too, at least. The aroma of the salmon from the oven was heavenly. She couldn't remember the last time she'd had fish, or the last time she'd been able to afford it.

"Oh, and let me pay you for the groceries. I'll give you what I have, but I won't be able to give you the rest until my next paycheck. I'm sorry, with the rent and every-thing…" She felt like an idiot, as he'd said not to worry.

"You know what? Just pay me when you get paid. No point leaving yourself short." He glanced up to her, and his expression should have put her at ease. He had kind eyes, along with the heat that seemed to rock between them in this kitchen. She had to tell herself the only reason she felt this way was because he was so nice and together and too good looking for his own good, so she turned her back to him, facing the gas range, which she was totally in love with. In fact, she loved this entire spacious, roomy kitchen.

"You mind if I ask you a personal question?" he said.

For a second, she feared what he'd ask, as she could see Shaunty in the living room, on the floor, with a coloring book open and crayons splayed around her, focusing on what she was doing and hopefully not listening in. She knew her daughter picked up on more than she should, which was why she'd left Shaunty's idiot father to try to give her a normal life. After nearly two years, she was still trying to figure out what that could be.

"Depends, I guess." She shrugged, wishing the water would hurry up so she could pour the macaroni in and make dinner. Then she and Shaunty could eat, and then what, go hide out in the bedroom? Gabriel's bedroom, actually, because he'd insisted on playing the gentleman after her dad broke the window. She stood there stiffly. She was damn sure he was going to ask her all about MM and how she could have hooked up with the likes of him. She was still wondering how she'd overlooked all his crazy shit just because he was tall, dark, and handsome and had an incredibly hot body. She reminded herself that in the beginning, he'd had a charm she didn't think she could live without. A sane person would have asked her if she'd had a head injury.

Gabriel tossed her another one of his killer smiles, the kind that lit up his face. "Well, I was wondering how you really are. You hit that car pretty hard, and even though you tried to hide it, I could see you were favoring that arm and your side." He gestured across the island with the knife he was holding. "If you're thinking it's best to ignore it, you could in fact be injured, and it wouldn't hurt to take a run to the emergency room and get an x-ray just to make sure. You know it's better to be safe."

That was exactly what she hadn't expected, exactly what she couldn't do, considering Medicaid wouldn't cover everything. "You know what?" she said. "I'm good, and that's not necessary. It only hurts a bit if I move too fast." She knew there would likely be a bruise on her arm, and maybe her hip too, and it might be a little uncomfortable for a few days, but she'd be fine. It was her pride that had been hurt more than anything.

Gabriel was taking her in, his eyes so bright. The color reminded her of a warm ocean, and confidence oozed from him, but she could also tell he didn't believe her, though he didn't say one word.

"Really, it's nothing," she said. "I'll be fine. I'm just embarrassed, is all. I'm sorry about what happened." She'd never experienced this kind of gentleness and caring from a man before.

He didn't smile and continued slicing up a cucumber. "So he found out where you lived and forced you to move because…" he started. Maybe he did have a right to know, considering MM would likely find her here and show up and become a royal pain in the ass. She wondered now whether Gabriel was having second thoughts.

"Because he doesn't take no for an answer. Because he

doesn't understand that it's over, that he's now crossing boundaries. All of that. He seems to think he can push and push and make me come back as if that will be all he has to do. He's not a man you can reason with, I'm sure you noticed," she added, waiting for him to question everything she'd done.

"So he's under the impression that you're with me, like together, in a relationship kind of way." Gabriel rested the knife on the wooden chopping block and swept the chopped cucumber up with his hand, then dumped it in the bowl with the rest of the greens.

She shrugged and wondered whether she should tell Gabriel that MM had broken a pizza delivery guy's nose two places ago when he'd shown up and assumed he was somehow involved with her. "He's under the impression that I've hooked up with some other man, because it's somehow impossible for me to stand on my own two feet, let alone want to. He thinks I've jumped into a relationship with another man when that's exactly the last thing I'm looking for. So, to answer your question, it probably did seem like we were together, and as you saw, he's not exactly the reasonable type. His first reaction is always jealousy and to see the worst, to overreact."

She took in Shaunty, so quiet, and wanted to take it all back, but then, she'd seen the worst of her father, and Elizabeth was pretty sure she didn't have a clue what normal was. She just hoped she hadn't screwed her up too much.

Shaunty glanced up and over to her. "Mom, he just wants you back—us back. He loves you, is all."

Damn! She sounded so reasonable. "I know, Shaunty. Hey, macaroni should be ready in about ten minutes. Why don't you clean up there, put your things away, and then go wash your hands?"

She noted that Gabriel said nothing else as her daughter cleaned up.

"So, mind if I ask you something?" she said. What was she doing? This wasn't supposed to be quid pro quo.

He brushed his hands together and then put the cutting board and knife beside the double farm sink as he started filling it with water. "Nope, shoot. Ask me anything."

She ripped open the macaroni box and pulled out the cheese packet before dumping the macaroni shells in the water and giving it a stir with a wooden spoon she'd pulled from the neatly organized drawer. "I've never met a man who eats so healthy. I mean, I noticed you don't have any packaged foods in the cupboards, except for a few containers of…" What was inside, she wasn't sure, because the clear Tupperware containers weren't labeled. The fridge didn't have any prepackaged dressings, condiments, or anything that a typical household jammed in there. It was so fresh that she was positive he shopped every day, or at least every other.

He wasn't smiling as he poured in dish soap and washed the knife, rinsed it off, and set it in the other sink. Then he washed the cutting board down, and it wasn't lost on her that he still hadn't said anything. She wished she'd asked nothing at all.

"I had leukemia as a kid," he said. He didn't turn around, and she froze with the wooden spoon, lost for words.

He squeezed out the sponge and then wiped the counter down where he'd been chopping vegetables, making everything so neat and tidy, another quality she'd never seen before in a man.

"I'm sorry, but you're okay now…? I mean, you look

great." Boy, that was exactly what she hadn't wanted to say.

He turned around, and it wasn't sadness she saw on his face but strength and a humor she hadn't expected. "Well, thanks. I think that's the first compliment you've given me." He continued to wipe the counter and then rested the sponge against the sink back before drying his hands.

Now she wondered, though, because he hadn't confirmed how he was doing. That had her alarm bells going off as she felt herself filling with empathy for him.

"But to answer your question, I'm fine," he said. "Completely healthy. Had a bone marrow transplant as a kid, just a few years older than Shaunty. Was good for a long time. Had a scare a few years back, but luckily it was nothing, just a false positive. It was enough for me to go all in with my health, though. Diet, exercise. I eat a really clean diet, no sugar, no white flour, limited healthy grains, and nothing processed ever, nothing from a box." He gestured to her box of macaroni, and for a second she wondered whether he was criticizing her in some way. She felt her jaw slacken.

"You know what? This is economics," she said. "I couldn't afford to eat that way, as much as I'd like to." The moment it left her lips, she wanted to take it back, even if it was true. It had sounded so defensive and made her sound like a shrew.

He walked around the island to her, his hands lifted. "There's no way I would ever criticize," he said. "I apologize if you took it that way. What I'm saying is I have to keep my body clean, otherwise it's a gamble I'm not willing to take, because I love life. You know, I spent some time getting serious after that last test, the one I thought would have me fighting another cancer. One of the things I learned is that the medical community has completely failed in some areas. The first thing a doctor should be asking when you walk into an exam room is 'What are you eating?' Except they can't, because they only study food for a few weeks even though we're consuming it every day and it affects our bodies. So I did my own homework, my own studying. I work out, and…" He stopped and let out a soft laugh as he looked down, and she realized the awkward moment. "I'm rambling, and your macaroni is probably done. You're right, though. It does cost a lot." He gestured and walked around to the wall oven, opened it, and pulled out his salmon.

She turned off the burner. There was nothing worse than overcooked macaroni. As she drained the pasta and went to add in some milk and the powdered cheese, she noticed Gabriel had dished up three bowls of salad. When she glanced over to him, he was watching her in a way that made her feel special, wanted, and she couldn't have that. Just as Shaunty raced into the kitchen, Gabriel said, "Hey, Shaunty, have you ever tried salmon?"

"No, is that fish?" her daughter asked.

Elizabeth squeezed the wooden spoon as she stirred in the clumps of processed orange powder and took in Gabriel scooping a small piece of fish on a plate and resting it on the counter with a fork. He pulled out one of the stools, and Shaunty climbed up and then looked over to her before taking a bite. "Is it okay, Mom?"

What the hell was she supposed to say? *No, don't eat it, because I don't want to be beholden to Gabriel any more than I am.* But she forced a smile to her face as she took in Gabriel dishing up his own plate before looking over to her. Then he did something she didn't expect: He held it out to her.

"Ah, Gabriel, thanks, but I made us dinner…" she started.

He glanced to Shanty, who was digging in to the

salmon.

"It's good, Mom," she said. "Have some."

She was about to say no when he did it again, that smile. "Elizabeth, I made more than enough. Please consider this a welcome to my home and thanks for moving in and renting a room from me. Come on, seriously, it's not a big deal."

Now why would he have to add that smile?

"Please," he added again, and she took in her daughter, who was watching her, the fork halfway to her mouth, and she didn't like the uncertainty she saw. Then she looked to the processed mac and cheese that had been on sale for seventy-five cents, and she knew she shouldn't.

"Okay, just this once, Gabriel. I'm serious. It's important that there are clear boundaries. I'm renting a room only. You're not cooking for me and Shaunty," she stated as she pulled out the stool beside Shaunty and sat at the island. Gabriel slid the plate of salmon and another fork in front of her along with a bowl of salad, and her mouth watered. She dug in and took a bite, and the taste was even better than she'd expected.

He lifted his hands as if her words could bite. "It's not a marriage proposal, Elizabeth. It's just sharing dinner. That's it. So just say thank you and…" He glanced over to her daughter, who was looking from him over to her. His expression was warm. "Don't read anything into it."

Okay, now she felt like a fool, and she just stared back at him until he finally looked away. She watched this very capable, strong, sexy, handsome, and incredibly fit man who'd opened his house to her as he pulled out a stool, sat down beside her daughter, and dug into his salad—but instead of seeing everything about him that was perfect, too perfect, she couldn't help worrying about what he was hiding.

Chapter Eight

"I'm sorry, Gabriel. There's nothing I can do," said Sheriff Blake Gatlin, a friend of his parents. "The law is the law, and no matter how much I'd like to bend it, I can't."

Blake had married Brandyne Parker, his parents' neighbor, a single mom of five, a good many years back. He had a hard square jaw that reminded Gabriel a lot of his father, deep eyes that seemed a mix of blue and green, and wavy light hair that was creased from where he'd settled his cowboy hat, which was now resting at the edge of his desk.

"So he's out, then," Gabriel said, feeling the vibration of his cell phone from the back pocket of his blue jeans. That would be the job site. His boss, Mic, a big man in his sixties, had white hair and a short fuse. He knew he would likely be wondering where he was. Even though he'd called and said he'd be a little late, he knew there was an expectation he'd be there first.

"Afraid so," Blake said. "Went before the judge, got slapped with a hundred-dollar fine, and..." He gestured in the air, his expression that of a man whose hands were tied. "If he shows up again, all we can do is haul him in, and hopefully if he goes in front of the same judge enough times, he'll get something a little stiffer. But let me ask you something. This woman who rented a room from you, this guy would be her ex? I'm not sure that's the kind of trouble you want on your doorstep. You may want to rethink the rental. If you need some help rectifying the situation and getting her to move on, you just have to ask."

Gabriel could feel the judgment coming from Blake as he stood before his desk, a beat-up old wood thing that was from another century, he thought. Blake was leaning back in his old squeaky chair, his hands now linked and folded over his belt, where his gun was holstered, his wedding ring flashing. He studied Gabriel as if he thought he was hiding something—or maybe that was just his imagination. Blake Gatlin was a cop first, and he had a way of talking as if he were questioning, studying.

"Yes, the guy's her ex, and your point here is what, exactly? I have no intention of kicking her to the curb," he added through gritted teeth, taking in the way the sheriff's lip quirked as if he found it funny, but he wasn't laughing. It was a look that said Gabriel was pushing it.

"What exactly do you know about this young lady? I mean, you sure you want this kind of headache? It may be more prudent to give her her money back and ask her to go. Otherwise, I hate to tell you, this guy could become a problem for you, the kind of thorn in your side that you don't want. It could likely cost you in ways you can't even begin to imagine."

There it was, the advice he didn't want.

"Look, Blake, seriously, I came to you because I thought I could actually get some help for Elizabeth. She's a nice lady, and she has a sweet little girl, smart. She doesn't deserve to have a dickhead like this dogging her heels. All I know is the last two places she's lived, he's found her and become a nuisance, and she's had to move. He wants her back and isn't taking no for an answer, and before you say she's the type who will eventually cave and just go back to him after he leaves a path of destruction for everyone else, I'll tell you she isn't. She's nice, just down on her luck and hasn't gotten a break. Instead of complaining about it, though, she's doing something about it. Doesn't that say something about a woman, when she won't stay with a loser like that but has the courage to stand up and say no and take her daughter to try to make a better life?"

"Fine," the sheriff said, leaning forward, slapping his hands on the desk, and giving him a look as if he were a pain in the ass. "I get it, I do. You know that. And it's admirable, you here, wanting to stick by her, but just make sure you're not doing it because of a pretty face. And…" He jabbed a finger his way. "You talk to your mom and dad, because I can't see Andy being too happy about any of this."

Great, here we go. The last thing he wanted or needed was for his dad to step in, because then he'd have to tell him why he'd rented out the room and explain why he wasn't about to ask his parents for a handout even though he knew his dad would bail him out of anything.

"You know what? This is my situation to deal with, not my dad's, and that's why I'm here. It's not my dad's problem to take care of for me. I'm a grown man who handles my own life. And again, Elizabeth is great. She doesn't deserve to be treated like this. She doesn't deserve to be messed with by this guy, so if there's any way you could maybe have a word with him, set him straight, tell him she isn't interested in him and to walk away and stop bothering her, I would really appreciate it. Maybe give him that tough-love cop talk about how he's pushed it and this is bordering on the kind of crazy stalkerish behavior that will land him in hot water and hard time. He needs to grow the fuck up and take the hints she's very clearly laid out to leave her the fuck alone, and then do so." Gabriel rested his hands on his hips, his cell phone buzzing again. He knew this time he couldn't ignore it, so he pulled it out and saw his boss's number.

"Fine, I'll have a word with Mac Murrin and set him straight, but you, sir, let your parents in on what's happened, because I don't want Andy Friessen in my face and on my doorstep, breathing down my neck, if, God forbid, this guy does show up at your house and takes a round out of you." Blake actually stood up and rested both palms on his desk, shaking his head. "You know as well as I do that your dad wouldn't stand for that, and since he's a friend of mine, I do not want that on my conscience. I do not want your dad angry at me, because…" He held up his hand when Gabriel went to interrupt him. "Go talk to your dad, tell him about Elizabeth, this ex of hers who's like a powder keg about to go off, and then I'll have a word with him."

Gabriel just stood there, squeezing his now silent phone, which had likely gone to voicemail again. Then he crossed his arms, taking in the expression on the sheriff's face as he walked around the desk and rested his hand on his shoulder.

"I get it," Blake said. "Really, I do, and I empathize with this woman and her situation, but we're talking about you, and the fact is that I know you and not her, and your dad would be pretty angry with me if he learned this shit was happening to you, that someone was messing with you, and I knew and didn't tell him. So when you leave here today, talk to your dad, and think about what I said, because if you insist on letting this young lady stay, then you need to be sure you at least got good locks on your doors and windows."

The expression on his face said it all, and Gabriel wanted to argue with him so he could…what? Understand Elizabeth and see her the way he did, as an amazing strong woman, even though her parents were eccentric and meddling, and she had a crazy ex, but her daughter was sweet, sharp, and smarter than most kids her age. Then there was Elizabeth herself, who seemed to have her head screwed on straight. If there was a black sheep in the oddball family he'd met, she was it.

"I hope I'm getting through to you, Gabriel. Talk to your dad," Blake repeated as he stepped away and opened his office door. "Then I'll personally go and have a talk with Mister Murrin."

That was all he could ask. "Thank you," he said as his phone started ringing again, and he stepped out of the sheriff's office and walked to the front door before pressing the phone to his ear. "Hello?"

"Where are you?" It was actually Dwayne, his boss's son, and he sounded irritated.

Gabriel stepped outside, seeing his truck, and jogged down the steps. "Just had to stop and take care of something, is all. Told your dad that when I left him a message. I'm on my way, will be there in less than five…"

"Hey, just giving you a heads up, we had some trouble here last night. Seems the job site was broken into. Kids, we think, spray painted everything, punched holes every-where, and the entire heating unit is trashed and has to be replaced. It's all hands on deck. The client is pissed, and dad even more so, because whoever was here last may not have locked up."

Gabriel stopped on the sidewalk in front of his pickup, pulling his keys from his pocket. He yanked open the door and just stood there a minute, lifting the phone away from his ear and staring at it. "I wasn't the last one there," he said, because this was that feeling he got when someone was about to pin something on him. He hoped he was wrong. "I left before you," he added.

"Did you? Oh, I don't remember that."

Oh, bullshit! There was no way in hell he was taking the fall. "Dwayne, cut the crap. You were finishing up the framing in the dining room when I walked out the door. You said you wanted it done because the electrician was coming in today. So that was you, and there's no way you're pinning it on me," he snapped. "Tell your dad I'm on my way."

He hung up, pocketed his phone, and climbed in his truck, then took a minute behind the wheel as he ran his hands roughly over his face and let out a breath. "Ah, fuck. Now what?" he said as he shoved the key in the ignition. It seemed today was just one thing after another, and things weren't going his way.

Chapter Nine

She'd spent the day unpacking the few boxes in her bedroom, where the air mattress was lying in a heap in the corner. A tiny hole she couldn't find made it absolutely useless to sleep on, but then, she and Shaunty had slept in Gabriel's very comfortable king-sized bed the night before, in a spacious room with a spa-like bathroom the likes of which she'd never seen.

She felt the need to set some boundaries. Where had he slept but on the sofa, a gentlemanly gesture that she couldn't let happen again, because after sharing that amazing, healthy, tasty dinner he'd cooked, she felt as if she was slipping into a place where she would and could become beholden to him, and she'd warned herself that nothing good ever came from owing anyone anything, especially a man as good looking and hot and charming as Gabriel Friessen.

It was a slippery slope, and the line could easily become blurred between them, considering she was living in his house. She'd promised herself that never again would she ever make the mistake of falling in love with a pretty face.

She was watching Shaunty, who was unpacking her dolls and putting them on a box she'd dressed up with an old blue paisley scarf, when there was a knock on the door to the house, followed by the doorbell ringing.

"Lizzie!" It was her mother calling out, followed by another series of raps and the doorbell ringing over and over.

"That's your granny at the door…" Elizabeth said as her daughter ran out and beat her there. The door was white, with a plexiglass front and a shiny deadbolt. She flicked it open, but her mom was still ringing. "Mom, seriously, I was coming," she said, taking in her mom's heavy makeup, blue shadow on her lids, with thick mascara and liner. Today she was in a yellow dress, sleeveless, from the looks of it, with a white sweater over her shoulders and a black shiny handbag. Her eyes, as always, scanned Elizabeth from head to toe, from her black and white T-shirt sundress, to her wet hair pinned up in a bun, to her bare feet. She was without a stitch of makeup.

"Oh, tish tosh," Chloe said. "And look at you, Lizzie. You need to finish your hair and put on some makeup, and that dress isn't flattering. Don't you have something nicer?" She stepped inside and was still talking about something, but Elizabeth didn't have a clue what.

Chloe walked straight for the kitchen. Just then, Elizabeth spotted her sister, Ruby, walking up the steps in a tank that was cut so low it left little of her cleavage to the imagination. Her hair was black with white streaks, and the shadow and liner around her eyes was thick and black. She was holding a shopping bag that seemed to have something pretty big in it.

"Hi, Ruby. What you got there?"

Her sister reeked of cigarette smoke, and Elizabeth was surprised she didn't have one lit up now and hanging out of her mouth. "New air mattress for you," Ruby said. "Mom said yours was a dud, wouldn't hold air last night, so I stopped at the store and picked one up for you and one for Shaunty, two singles that were on sale." Ruby handed the bag to her, and Elizabeth watched as her sister took in the porch and the house and then whistled. "Wow, look at this! Looks like you scored big time here. This is nice. And mom said that the guy who owns it is a hottie."

She had to fight the urge to roll her shoulders. It was just a quirk of her family's, the way they always had to stick their noses into every aspect of her life, and they had an odd way of viewing people, slotting them into categories as if that meant anything.

"Thanks for the air mattresses," she said. "Come on in." She forced herself not to elaborate on Gabriel or this house, and she closed the door, hearing her mom and Ruby in the kitchen with Shaunty. She found she needed to take another breath and let it out.

"So where's all the furniture? A sofa and big screen, very important, but there's nothing else in here." Ruby gestured as she walked around. Her boots had a three-inch heel, and her jeans were skintight, likely a size 12 on her size 14 frame.

"I told you already," Chloe started, "that he put all he had into this house, into renovating. The furniture he's planning on buying next."

Of course her mom knew everything, Elizabeth thought. She'd been poking and prodding and being extremely intrusive as she questioned Gabriel the day before.

"Oh, right, and didn't you tell me too that his dad owns a ranch west of town?"

He did? She just took in her mom and the way she nodded. "Yup, big family he comes from. His parents live outside of town, and he has two brothers and two sisters. One of the pairs are twins. He still helps his dad out on the ranch with the cattle, a big venture for the two of them, and he splits his time between that and construction. The construction he got into to learn everything he needed to fix this house. He's a thinker." Her mom tapped her forehead with her fingers. "And he really is a useful feller. Has a good family, just the kind of man you should be setting your sights on." Her mom nodded, and Elizabeth wondered what expression was on her face, because she didn't know anything about Gabriel.

"You know I don't agree with Mom on much, but he sounds like a great catch," Ruby added, and at this point Elizabeth knew there was nothing she could say to get it into their minds that this was platonic and there would never be a boyfriend–girlfriend or any kind of relationship between them. So she said nothing.

"And how are things going with mister hottie?" Her mom was now picking up the kettle that was tucked beside the coffeemaker—and that was another thing. Gabriel had left half a pot of fresh coffee for her to drink that morning. There'd been a note that said, *No sense wasting it. Drink it.* She'd had to fight the urge to crumple the note but instead had folded it up and dumped it in the trash. Then, after her shower, she'd dug through the garbage and pulled it out before tucking it into the box of keepsakes and stuff in her room.

"His name is Gabriel, Mom. Seriously, don't call him that. Even though, yes, I admit, he is handsome, that doesn't define who a person is."

Her mom gave her an odd look, and she took in Shaunty, who was sitting at the counter on a stool. There was a bag of chocolate chip cookies there. Of course her mom had brought them. That was just a normal everyday part of being an Abercrombie: Cookies and candy were always out.

"Oh, come on, Lizzie, spill!" Ruby said. "I'm so pea-green jealous with envy, hearing all about Gabriel from Mom and how you scooped him up, and he owns this? Wow, this is a step up for you." She was leaning on the kitchen island, reaching into the bag of cookies. She handed one to Shaunty and took two for herself, and Chloe was plugging in the kettle and opening cupboard doors and drawers looking for what, exactly? She didn't have a clue.

"Ruby, seriously, there's nothing to tell, and I didn't scoop anyone. I'm merely renting a room from a nice man in a house. That's it. There's nothing more to it, so don't make it into something it isn't. Mom, what are you doing?" She glanced from her sister to her mom before she pulled out a stool beside Shaunty and reached for the bag, grabbed one of the chocolate chip cookies, looked at it, and then took a bite.

"Well, tea bags, of course. My my, I've just never seen anything this organized. This just is not normal for a man," her mom commented.

"I have no tea, Mom, and you're not going through Gabriel's things. Remember, I rent a room from him. We're not living together. His stuff, my stuff. Boundaries. Tea wasn't on the list of essentials for me." No, tea was way down under…well, she'd have to get a better job, more hours, and better pay.

"Well, why didn't you tell me? I could have brought you over some of my Red Rose. But I'm sure Gabriel wouldn't mind if you used his tea. It's the right thing for a man to do." Her mom gave her all of her attention. The way she looked at her, it was as if she was getting ready to lay in and tell her something really important. "You know, Elizabeth, you could do worse than Gabriel, and I'm telling you there's interest there. With guys, you have to let them do things for you. They like to provide for a woman. Men don't like all that independence and boundaries stuff you keep going on and on about. Yes, you made a doozy of a mistake with MM. Didn't we point that out to you?" Her mom was pulling open all the cupboards again and then stopped and faced her, a puzzled expression on her face. "His cupboards are empty. He's got nothing, no cereal, potato chips, cookies, crackers… What if he gets hungry? That's just no way for anyone to live."

Her sister started laughing. Crumbs from the cookies were all over the neat and tidy island. Then her mom was in the fridge again, looking around at all the healthy greens, fresh vegetables, fruit. She closed the fridge as if she'd been defeated. "This is just so wrong, Lizzie. He doesn't even have real food here. What kind of man is he?"

For a second, she didn't know what to say. She had to remind herself that her mom was serious, but then, she knew well her mom's idea of cooking was to throw a couple TV dinners in the oven and voila! A complete balanced meal in one serving.

"Gabriel likes to eat healthy." She bit into her cookie, knowing he'd never consider eating one of these, and for a second she had to fight the urge to read the list of ingredients, because once she did, she knew she'd never let her daughter have another bite. Then she realized by the odd look on her mom's face that she didn't get it. "You know, fresh foods, vegetables, fish, lean meats? Healthy stuff, no additives, no preservatives, no stuff with zero nutrition." She picked up the bag of cookies as if to make a point and set it back down.

Her mom pulled back as if she'd just realized Gabriel was from another place in the universe and what Elizabeth had said made no sense. "He one of those tree huggers who's always eating granola and such?" she said as the kettle boiled. She unplugged it, of course. She didn't have a choice, since there were no tea bags.

"No, he just takes his health seriously, and he's a good cook, too."

"Yeah, he made me and Mom dinner last night, salmon and salad," Shaunty added as she took a bite of cookie, letting the crumbs drop on the counter.

"Do say!" Ruby said. "He made you dinner? That doesn't sound like a man who wants boundaries. Just the opposite there, Lizzie."

She wished they'd stop calling her Lizzie and call her Elizabeth, a serious name. "He was just being nice, is all, a first dinner here." She hoped to steer the conversation somewhere else. To anything else.

"And he paid for Mom's groceries because she didn't have enough," Shaunty said. Elizabeth leveled her daughter with a sharp glance, and her expression was priceless. "Oh. I wasn't supposed to say anything, was I?"

Chloe and Ruby were now gawking as if they'd just been given everything. "So let me get this straight. He bought your groceries…"

"I'm paying him back. I was a little short, is all," she interrupted.

"And he let me and Mom sleep in his bed last night. It was really comfortable."

Ruby handed Shaunty another cookie. "You don't say. Oh, tell me everything, my sweet little niece."

Shaunty giggled. It was a sweet sound, but at the same time, Elizabeth wanted to keep her stuff private. Her family didn't seem to get the simple concept of boundaries.

"Ruby, Mom, stop that," she said. "None of that means anything. He's just a nice man and felt bad…"

"And Daddy showed up and wanted to hurt him. The cops came, and…" Shaunty stopped and looked up to her, and she could feel her mom's and Ruby's gazes burning into her. She glanced over to them, and yup, this was the first time she'd seen them speechless. The expression on their faces was priceless.

"MM showed up here?" Ruby gestured to the counter. Her mom still had her mouth open and was leaning on her hands, both palms pressed on the island in her overly dramatic way.

"No, at the grocery store," Elizabeth said. "Well, rather, the parking lot, as I was getting into Gabriel's pickup, and he did what MM always does. He overreacted and thought Gabriel and I were *together* together, you know, which is none of his business anyway." She glanced down at her daughter. "Your dad just has to learn that it's over and we're not coming back."

"So why the cops?" Ruby asked. Her mom, though, seemed to have composed herself.

"He tried to hit Gabriel," Elizabeth said. "I tried to stop him and grabbed his arm, and I somehow got propelled into a parked car. I'm fine." She lifted her hand. "But Gabriel called the cops, and they took MM away. That's all I know about it. Haven't heard from him again."

"Maybe it's time Marty goes and has a talk with MM," Ruby said.

Elizabeth wanted to roll her eyes at her sister's suggestion, but just then she heard footsteps, and the front door opened. There was Gabriel, wearing blue jeans, a faded shirt, and his work boots. The expression on his face was priceless. She could just imagine what he was thinking, as she knew everyone was staring at him.

"Hello," he said and reached down to untie his work boots and kick them off.

"Lizzie was just telling us that you had a run-in with MM last night?" Of course her mom didn't know discretion.

"And I'm Ruby, Lizzie's older sister. She was just filling me in on what a gentleman you are, cooking dinner and giving her your bed. I swear men like you have all but disappeared." Her sister actually met Gabriel halfway to the kitchen, really giving him an eyeful of her generous bust, and Elizabeth wanted to hide her face, wishing Ruby would shut the hell up and stop.

"Nice to meet you, Ruby." He was polite, and then he gave Elizabeth all of his attention. "I wanted to have a word with you about MM," he said, but he didn't say anything. He walked closer and stopped a respectable distance away, taking in the bag of cookies and likely the crumbs, but then his beautiful eyes, which didn't hold a bit of craziness, fell on her. "I'm just going to grab a shower first and wash off all this sawdust and grit. Then maybe we can talk."

"Sure," she said, sitting on the stool. She watched him nod politely to her mom and sister and then walk down the hall, where she heard a door close, and she let out a breath, not realizing she'd been holding it. When she glanced over to her mom and sister, she realized they didn't miss any of it.

"So again, Lizzie, how is any of this just a guy and girl sharing space?" Ruby said. "Because, got to say, the heat was absolutely scorching from the chemistry between you two the minute he walked through the door, the minute he laid eyes on you from across the room. You can tell yourself you're not interested, but I can tell you your face is telling a different story." She opened her purse and pulled out her wallet, then yanked out what looked like a hundred dollars and tossed it on the counter. "And if you're short on money, you just got to ask. Okay, Mom, we should go. I told Gary I'd meet him at the Triple Wave for happy hour and the two-dollar wings tonight."

All she could do was stare at the cash on the counter and watch as her sister and mom talked nonstop as they walked out the door, and she looked down to her daughter, who was watching her as if waiting for her to tell her what was happening next.

"How about we blow up those air mattresses and get our beds made, and then you and me can figure out what's for dinner?" Elizabeth said.

She watched as her daughter climbed off the stool, grabbed the bag of mattresses Ruby had brought, and started dragging it to their bedroom. Then she took in the crumbs scattered over the counter and reached for a sponge at the sink. She wiped up all the crumbs, picked up the cash her sister had tossed down on the counter, and tucked it in her back pocket. She stuck the bag of cookies in the cupboard with the few dry goods she had.

At the same time, she stared at the front door her sister had just walked through and then shook her head, because there was no way there would ever be anything between her and Gabriel. She'd been down that road before, and she had no intention of going there again with anyone who looked as good as he did. Nope, this roomy situation would stay just like that, platonic, renting a room, and staying out of each other's way. If she put her mind to it, it would be easy.

Chapter Ten

S he was absolutely gorgeous, the way she was sitting cross legged, her cheeks puffed out, her lips around the plastic nozzle as she blew up a single air mattress. Shaunty was making up a bed with a second mattress as Gabriel stood in the doorway, watching the mother and daughter and trying to figure out what was wrong with this picture, as he couldn't see how Elizabeth fit with Mac Murrin. It was just one of those images that didn't work.

"Hey there, so how was work today?" she asked. He hadn't realized she was done blowing up the mattress and was pushing the plastic valve in.

"Work... It was one of those ridiculous days that I'd like to forget. There was a break-in at the job site overnight, some vandalism, and most of the work we did has to be redone," he said, and he took in the way her eyes widened.

She stood up, resting the air mattress on the ground and moving it over to the wall with her foot. "Shaunty, can you make up both beds? I'm going to start dinner," she said and then walked over to him and gestured out into the hall.

He followed her into the living room, and he wasn't sure what to make of how tense she appeared and the expression on her face.

"Do they know who caused the damage?" she said.

He shook his head, because he was still trying to shake off how Dwayne had tried to allude to the fact that he'd been the last to leave and forgot to lock up. The first thing Gabriel had done as he'd walked into the mess of what looked like teenage hoodlums gone wild was set the record straight with Mic that his son had still been wrapping up when he left. Then the cops had been there, and it was likely insurance would kick in to cover the cleanup and rebuild.

"No. Could've been some kids, by the looks of it. Kind of what happens when someone forgets to lock up." Yeah, he was still pissed at Dwayne and had noted the way he'd made a point of avoiding Gabriel the rest of the day, which made it difficult on a job site, where they basically had torn apart what they'd already done to start all over again.

Elizabeth was standing there with her hands linked together in front of her, her amber eyes lacking the confidence and strength he'd come to associate with who she was. "Are you sure it wasn't MM?" The way she said it, he realized why she was looking at him the way she was, as if she was somehow responsible.

"Oh, I see. That's what that was." He gestured and walked into the kitchen, where he pulled open the fridge and reached for a can of coconut water. He cracked the top and took a glass from the cupboard to pour it in, taking in how she now lingered on the other side of the counter.

"I'm not sure of your meaning."

Even the way she frowned was priceless.

"So let me get this straight," he said. "I have a break-in at my job site, and you somehow think your ex could be responsible?" He shouldn't do it, but he couldn't resist teasing her.

Even the way her brows furrowed was attractive. "No, I just thought the timing was weird, is all—and yes, it's something he'd do. I wouldn't put it past him. I would feel responsible," she said, and there it was, the guilt. It was just a second that he saw it, and then it passed as she composed herself.

He shook his head and took a swallow of the coconut water, then held up the remainder in the can to her. She just shook her head. "No, but thank you," she said.

"Well, it wasn't him, and even if it was, it's not on you. You're not responsible for him. Besides, he was only released this morning after appearing in front of a judge and being slapped with a hundred-dollar fine. How would he even know where I worked? That would be quite a stretch if he did. Regardless, I wanted to talk with you about him being out and what that means," he said. She stiffened and said nothing. "I've got a new window coming tomorrow for your room, but for now, make sure the doors and windows stay locked in the rest of the house." Evidently, what he said was exactly what she hadn't been expecting, by the expression on her face.

"That's it? That's all you wanted to say about it?" Okay, now she not only sounded confused, she looked confused.

"What were you expecting me to say?"

She pushed away from the counter, and he took in the loose T-shirt dress she was wearing, her messy bun, and how gorgeous she was. He supposed there was nothing that wouldn't look fantastic on her.

"Well, that you didn't sign up for this trouble and

you've had a chance to rethink it, and I half expected you to tell me and Shaunty to go. I still do." She stopped pacing and stood with her arms hanging loosely at her sides.

He put down his glass and walked around the counter. "Now that would really make me a scumbag, and I'm not that. But since we're talking about him, let's talk about him. He's Shaunty's father, so he's in her life, and he sees her, which means he's going to be coming here. You said the last few places he wouldn't leave you be."

She crossed her arms, and it wasn't lost on him that she didn't resemble her sister at all. Ruby, that was her name, was a different version of their mother, and then there was Elizabeth. "I see where this is going," she said. "Well, you can rest assured MM will not be getting the address to this house. He wants to see her, I take her to him, but that doesn't happen often." She firmed her lips, and he could see talking about this guy was a sore spot for her.

"Okay, but still, that's no way to live. I know you told that cop you spoke with someone about a restraining order, but I think speaking to an actual lawyer and getting something that forces him to stay away from you would be prudent. I can get the name of someone good…"

She lifted her hand, and he could see the minute she was done listening. "Stop. That isn't going to happen, because I can't afford a lawyer. They cost, remember, and he's never threatened me. He just doesn't understand that it's over and has been now for a long time. It's a harmless, annoying…" She stopped talking and crossed her arms again, and he could see her thinking. "Okay, I would love it if he would stop, but I've exhausted my options, and I'm not about to say he did something when he didn't just to find a way to conform to some law and get him to stop bugging me."

He didn't think he'd ever heard anyone with such strong convictions. "You know what? I really do admire that you won't let anyone convince you to make something up to get what you need to happen, but I think talking to a real lawyer may give you more options. With most lawyers, there's a free consult first. You get the right info and then go from there." He knew she was about to argue again, and he couldn't resist reaching out and touching her arm. "Seriously, stop. Just humor me. You can talk to my dad's attorney. It's just a talk. You're not committing to anything. Being my dad's lawyer, that means someone really good."

She took a second to consider and then raised a brow. "Talk only, but I'm serious, Gabriel. I don't have…" She stopped talking, and he knew how cash strapped she was.

"I know it's the cost, but you're just talking, free consult, remember?" He'd maybe have a word first with his dad's lawyer, see if anything could be done easily. "And I spoke with the sheriff this morning. He's going to have a word with MM. Maybe between him and the lawyer, this guy can be convinced to go away and leave you alone."

She inclined her head. "Well, that would make it easy, but don't get your hopes up, Gabriel, because I'm resigned to the fact that my poor choice in men has landed me a pain in the ass that I'll be stuck with forever. It definitely is a lesson well learned that falling in love is for fools." Then her daughter raced into the kitchen before he could say anything to convince her how wrong she was.

"All done, so what are we making for dinner?" Shaunty said.

Gabriel watched as Elizabeth gave all her attention to her daughter, and he was stuck on the fact that she had closed the door on any opportunity for love with someone good. As he watched this woman who'd walked into his house with this precocious girl, he couldn't help thinking of the fun he would have changing her mind. But how? That was something he'd have to think on.

Chapter Eleven

"He showed up here yesterday, came in looking angrier than a stirred-up nest of hornets," said Margie, Elizabeth's coworker at the automotive parts store. "He demanded to know where you lived now, and Barry had to go out and tell him we don't have that kind of personal information on you, and if we did, we wouldn't tell him anyway. He didn't seem happy with that, though, and Barry had to pick up the phone and tell him he was calling the cops if he didn't leave," she added in a low whisper that was still loud enough that if anyone else had been at the counter, they'd have heard.

Margie was reed thin, with straight brown hair, and she had four inches on Elizabeth. She wore a red vest, the standard uniform for everyone who worked behind the counter, and it did nothing for her except make her look like a scarecrow. Elizabeth had only tucked her purse under the front counter at the back of the shop before Margie had informed her of the previous day's visit from MM. Of course he wasn't going to go away.

"So is Barry here?" she asked, feeling her heartbeat

kick up, because she knew MM was putting her job in jeopardy, and she couldn't help worrying Barry would tell her that was it and she'd have to find another job.

"In back, but don't worry none. I'm sure it's fine."

She wasn't so sure, but she should have known he'd show up. Maybe Gabriel was right about the lawyer, and maybe after talking to said lawyer, she'd have a plan and some direction, something with teeth that would help her find a way to make MM go away and stop this craziness.

"Hey, Elizabeth, you got a second?" Barry appeared from the open door to the back office. She took in his round face and expanding middle, his glasses, and his dark hair, a mix of gray and black. For a second, she felt the floor beneath her feet soften.

"Of course," she said as she pulled at her red vest and, on instinct, tucked her long dark hair behind her ears. She stepped into his office, and he closed the door behind her. She just stood there, seeing through the glass to where Margie was talking with a customer who'd stepped up to the counter. "Margie was just filling me in on yesterday, that MM showed up and caused a scene," she said. "I'm sorry about that."

Her heartbeat kicked up again, but he lifted his hand as if it were no big deal and then perched on the edge of the steel desk. Papers were stacked in a box on the other side, and the corkboards in his office had invoices and papers pinned everywhere.

"That's not on you, Elizabeth, and it's not really your fault, but he is affecting business coming in, and customers. I won't hesitate to call the cops and press charges if he shows up again."

She lifted her hands. "Of course, and you should."

Then he glanced down at the desk, and she had an

awful feeling. It was something in how he appeared so uneasy and in what he wasn't saying.

"You know how bad I feel about having to cut your hours down to half time. If I could give you more, I would, but the reality is that my costs and overhead are going up, yet my prices and profit are going down. It's forcing me to make tough choices I don't want to make. I want to give you some warning that I'm cutting hours again at the end of the month—"

"What?" she said, interrupting him.

He lifted his hand, shaking his head. "I'm sorry, Elizabeth. Truly, I am. Unless business picks up, starting the end of the month, I can only put you on the schedule for Saturdays and give you the opening shift until noon. I'll understand if you say no, I would, but my hands are tied. Again, I didn't want to hit you with that at the last minute when you have no options," he said.

Her heart sank as she tried to figure out what one three-hour shift a week was going to pay for. Nothing. "Barry, I have rent to pay, a daughter to feed." Of course, it sounded as if she was pleading, because she really was.

"Again, I'm sorry, and that's why I'm telling you now, because of how bad I feel. I wish things were different, and …"

For the first time, she could really feel his sincerity and how much this was bothering him. She let out a breath. This wasn't an easy choice. "Okay, thanks for letting me know."

Suddenly, he stood up, and she didn't know what had him looking through the glass behind her. She turned, and there at the counter, bumping in front of another customer, was MM.

"Oh no," she said and opened the door, hearing Barry behind her.

"There she is," MM snapped. "I want to talk to you, Lizzie, right now." He slapped his hand on the counter, making an awful sound, and Elizabeth could feel her face burn as she became the center of everyone's attention.

"Keep your voice down," she said in a low voice that was laced with an edge she hoped he got. "This is where I work, and you coming in here and causing a scene has to stop."

But his eyes, the blue she'd once been a sucker for, were cold and unfeeling. Thankfully, they no longer did anything for her except have her wondering what she'd been thinking at the time, not understanding how she could have fallen for Mac Murrin and stayed with him as long as she had.

"Elizabeth…" Barry stepped in, and she took in the compassion in his face. She wouldn't have blamed him one bit if he decided to let her go right now.

"Barry, it's fine. I'll get rid of him," she pleaded, and for a minute she wondered whether he'd argue, but he inclined his head.

She stepped around the counter and put her hand on MM's arm, pulling him with everything she had away from the only customer, who wore a disbelieving expression. To make it worse, she could feel everyone's eyes on her still, and it was the worst feeling. She stepped into one of the aisles where the smaller boxes of parts were by the front door, blocking everyone's view.

"Okay, you need to listen very carefully."

"No." He stuck his head closer to her, his nose nearly bumping hers. "No, you listen to me, Lizzie. I've had enough of this. You think you get to hook up with some other guy on me and then send some sheriff to come tapping on my door, trying to tell me how it's over with my girlfriend? I think not."

She was staring at him, because it was always the same, except this time she was stuck on the sheriff part. "Wow, I never expected that. The sheriff really paid you a visit?" Okay, maybe calling the cops had been a great idea on Gabriel's part.

"Look, I'm willing to forget all of this, to let this all go and move on. Come home, where you belong, where my daughter belongs. This has gone on long enough, and the fact that you can't seem to forgive isn't boding too well for your character, Lizzie. Then there's this." He was in a faded blue shirt with a tear in the shoulder, a spot of grease from an engine he'd likely been working on, and faded blue jeans. He lifted up the shirt, showing his fabulous abs —and a giant tattoo across his stomach that read *Lizzie*. She was positive her jaw dropped. Was he insane?

"You tattooed my name across your stomach?" She realized too late how loud she was, and she slapped her hand over her mouth as he dropped his shirt, a big goofy grin on his face. He reached into his pocket, where the chain had once dangled, and pulled out a small velvet box. When he popped it open, a ring with a sizable rock glittered inside, and for a second she had to remind herself to breathe. Then he got down on one knee, and she could feel the horror of the moment. *This can't be happening.*

"Lizzie, I should have done this before, and if I had, we'd likely not be here now, so marry me. You're a part of me, and you're branded on me now for everyone to see, everyone to know." That was it. That was all he said as he stared at her with hopeful eyes.

"MM, get up right now." She touched his arm and pulled him, and he smiled that charming flashy smile that was both goofy and downright sexy, but the only thing it did for her now was tighten her resolve. She had to figure out a way to get him to go away and leave her be. "This isn't happening," she said. "This will never happen. I am not marrying you, and the fact that you went and tattooed my name across your abs just shows how you're beginning to lose your grip on the reality of the situation. You're not hearing me. It also shows how desperate you are, which should terrify me."

She snapped the box he was still holding closed, taking in the moment she'd dashed his hopes, his joy. With his volatile, unpredictable personality, this was where she had gone wrong. She crossed her arms and knew the look she leveled on him was far from friendly.

"Okay, listen up," she said, "because you're not getting the message. It's over. It's been over a long time between us, since I walked out the door nearly two years ago after having enough of your shenanigans. You just don't get it, and maybe I'm not being clear, so here it is: Leave me alone. We're done. I'm not coming back ever. I don't love you anymore. I have no feelings left for you. Every time I see you now, I'm afraid of what you'll do, and I want to run the other way. There is no chance in hell that you'll get me back, ever, and that tattoo just shows you're seriously delusional, because we are so done.

"That sheriff who paid you a visit is one hundred percent correct about you needing to stop," she continued. "No more showing up where I work, no more showing up where I live. You will leave me alone and not come back here again, and whoever I choose to see and date is not your business. We're not together, and in fact, if you keep pushing these big dramatic displays, I'll be forced to consult a lawyer and go before a judge and get a restraining order so the next time the cops are called, you'll be locked up. Am I being clear enough for you? Is there anything I said just now that you still don't understand clearly? We are finished. You need to move on and find yourself someone new to date, because we will never, ever be together again."

Oh, man, she was proud of herself, and she wanted to pat herself on the back. Except she didn't know what to expect from the way he was glaring at her now. She wasn't about to cower or back down, though.

"You owe me," he said as he stuffed the ring box back in his pocket, and for a second she almost laughed before she realized he was serious.

"And what exactly do I owe you for?" she said. He couldn't seriously expect her to reimburse him for his last Hail Mary to win her back—but then, this was MM. Of course he could.

She could see him thinking. It was in his expression, the immature way he made a face before he said, loud enough for everyone to hear, "For forcing me to get a vasectomy so I didn't knock you up again."

She heard something drop and looked up, over the shelf, seeing Barry there, his eyes wide, and she just wanted to crawl into a hole from the embarrassment.

Chapter Twelve

Gabriel had just lifted the handle and lowered the tailgate of his pickup when he spotted his dad's new black Silverado pull up behind him. Andy Friessen was wearing dark shades, and he had a way of looking at Gabriel even through the windshield that had him feeling that his father had something on his mind, was going to address something with him, and he didn't have a clue what it was, because he was giving nothing away. It was unnerving at times, especially when he knew something Gabriel didn't want him to know. Growing up, that was never a position he'd wanted to be in with his dad.

Andy was the kind of man people didn't take advantage of, which had been fantastic for his children, his family, but at the same time, he didn't let any of his kids get away with anything. Gabriel knew and understood better than most that Andy would walk through fire and hell for every one of them without a single thought for his own well-being.

His dad took his time stepping out of his pickup, shutting the door, and looking across the street to the neighbors' bungalow as if they were outside waiting. Then he strode over to Gabriel, his legs looking long in dark jeans and a navy shirt with the sleeves rolled up to show his strong forearms. He was still so fit, confident of who he was, the kind of man he knew, as his mother had commented a few times, women wanted. His dark hair was neatly cut, with threads of gray, and he seemed to be working a piece of gum.

"Didn't know you were coming by," Gabriel said, resting his hand on the back of the open flatbed where the new window he'd just picked up on credit was lying nestled in Styrofoam so he could install it in Elizabeth and Shaunty's room. This time, he'd made sure to check the latch to see that it wasn't defective.

His dad said nothing for a minute, then pulled off his shades and tucked them in his shirtfront. His icy blue eyes were etched in lines now as he squinted down at Gabriel. He was so tall, at six two, and he was reminded of how much he'd always wanted to be just like his dad, who'd been a hero to him ever since he was a little kid.

"So I heard you had some trouble," Andy said.

Ah, right, he was supposed to talk to his parents, or that was what Blake had said. Guess he didn't need to now. "So the sheriff called you, huh?" He tried not to smile as he shook his head.

"Oh, I think Blake was under the impression that you and I had already had a conversation, but yes, he told me about the parking lot fiasco where you almost got your ass kicked over some girl." The way his dad said it, he knew he was misunderstanding everything. "We had Blake and Brandyne over for dinner last night, and the conversation just drifted there naturally. Of course, he realized his mistake from my reaction and your mom's. You'd actually shared none of those facts—that someone who could be a little dangerous had tried to hurt and mess with you and that you visited him to do something to help this girl."

He knew there was more from the way his dad was watching him and glancing out across the road again. "And Mom sent you, right?"

This time, his dad did smile. "The only thing that stopped her from driving in this morning was the fact that I reminded her you're working on a construction crew at dawn, and having your mother show up on the job and pull you aside was exactly what you wouldn't want, because you're old enough to stand on your own two feet and make your own decisions and you don't need us to step in and fix something that I can only presume you've already taken care of."

He couldn't remember his dad ever saying so much, and for a second he just stared at him, wondering what else there was, because there was always a what else with his dad. He just didn't share things with everyone, keeping more to himself, which was unsettling.

"So you're telling me you settled Mom down by convincing her I'm handling this and it isn't a problem, yet here you are."

His dad didn't smile. He only pulled in a deep breath and glanced toward Gabriel's house, then back to him. "It doesn't work that way. See, even though you're grown and moved on, we're still your parents and will always worry and wonder if you're okay. It's our right, so I told your mom I would stop by and pay you a visit and have a sit-down with you about what was going on and make sure this isn't something serious—and, more to the point, that you've taken care of it."

Great, this sounded as if the conversation was about to go in a direction he didn't want it to go, with his dad getting into his personal business and finding out all the things he didn't want to share. He pulled in a breath, taking in the sound of a motorcycle. The loud roar of the Harley was coming closer, and that had his dad turning and taking a look. All Gabriel could think of was *Why now? Why right fricking now would crazy-ass Marty be showing up here?*

Gabriel stood there and just watched as Elizabeth's brother pulled in front of his truck, and he took in the way his dad studied everything about the man before turning that burning, intense gaze back on Gabriel. That gaze wouldn't let him slip away, pinning him where he was until his dad had every answer he wanted.

Andy gestured toward Marty. "Friend of yours?"

Gabriel took in the window lying in the back of his pickup, which he wanted to get in the house and get installed. Then he wanted to make some dinner and chill out for an hour or so, but instead he took in Marty getting off his bike and taking off his helmet, wearing what looked like the exact grubby getup he'd seen him in before, his face appearing as if he hadn't shaved in days.

"Hey, there," he said with that smoker's raspy voice as he strode over to them, walking with his hands at his sides, much like a gorilla.

"Marty, this is my dad, Andy Friessen." He gestured, and his dad extended one hand to the biker dude. They were the same height, but Marty was bigger all around.

He took in the exchange between the two and knew, without Andy even looking his way, that his dad had likely a hundred questions, if not more.

"So how do you know my son?" he said.

Oh, here we go.

"Your son rented a room to my sister and niece. Hey, listen, wanted to stop by and was hoping you could give this to Lizzie for me." Marty pulled an envelope from his pocket, and it didn't take a genius to figure out it had a bunch of cash in it. Of course, his dad was staring at it, and his face, his entire expression, darkened. Then he turned all of it on Gabriel, but he didn't say anything, as if waiting for Gabriel to say something to enlighten him on this situation, which didn't look good.

"I can," he said, but he didn't hold out his hand as he stared at the envelope being held out to him. He figured from the way his dad was staring at him that he needed to ask more. "Is that a bunch of cash?" he finally said.

"She's had some tough breaks. It's to help her out," Marty replied.

Gabriel took the envelope and tucked it into his back pocket. "I'll see that she gets it," he said.

Marty was still there. He hadn't left. "And just let Lizzie know, about the MM situation, I'm on it, and I'll handle it. Great to see he didn't mess you up. He's been known to put a person in the hospital with that temper of his." Marty reached over and slapped his shoulder, then fisted his hand in front of him, and Gabriel wasn't sure how to respond. Marty then walked away and was back on his bike, revving the loud thing and pulling away.

This was the first time he'd ever seen his dad speechless. Then Andy said, his hands now resting on his hips and giving Gabriel his full attention, "So what the hell is going on, and who is this Lizzie?"

"Elizabeth is her name, and I rented a room to her. She's a nice lady with a little girl," Gabriel said.

His dad couldn't seem to form a word as he looked up the street to where the bike had gone and gestured with his thumb.

"Yeah, okay, I'm seeing what you're thinking, but she doesn't fit with that image." What else could he say? He still couldn't understand, after meeting her family, how she'd turned out almost normal. Whatever that meant.

"Let me get this straight. You have a roommate, a woman with a child, who's living in your house and paying you money to rent a room from you." His dad lifted his hand, and he knew there was still more he wanted to say, so he said nothing. "Why?"

Okay, there it was, the reason he hadn't wanted his parents to know. "Well, was short on cash. The renovations ended up costing me way more than I expected and kind of put me in a hole, so…" He stopped talking, because he could see the way his dad was leaning in with his energy, his arms crossed, waiting for him to finish. His dad's burning intensity held him in place and made him feel as if he were under a microscope and there was no hope of slipping away.

"So you opened your home to a stranger because you're broke," Andy said.

"Yup, that would be it." He tapped his hand on the tailgate, seeing that his dad was trying to figure out what to say.

"And you couldn't come to me."

Gabriel just stared at his dad and wondered how to explain to him that asking for help just wasn't something he could do. "No, I couldn't. This is my problem, mine to fix, and if I come running to you, what does that say about my ability to handle things? So no, Dad, I'm not taking any handouts," he said. He wasn't really sure how his dad was going to respond, but Andy seemed to relax and uncrossed his arms.

"Well, okay then. But answer me this. Is this Lizzie…"

"Elizabeth," he said.

"Sorry, Elizabeth. Is she the girl who was at the center of you almost getting your ass kicked?" His dad reached over and squeezed his shoulder, likely because he couldn't hide how defensive he was feeling. "Just humor me and maybe fill me in on what's going on. The girl…"

"Lady," Gabriel said, and this time crossed his arms, as he didn't miss the twitch tugging at the corners of his dad's lips.

"Excuse me. Okay, I think I'm starting to get the picture a little clearer. I take it she's the one at the center of this."

Gabriel nodded. "But it's not as you think. It's about a guy she's been done with for a long time who won't leave her be. She's a nice lady, she has a great kid, and she just needs a break." Why did it feel like he was having to defend Elizabeth to his father?

"Well, that's mighty noble, but it's starting to sound as if you have feelings you shouldn't for this woman, and from what I've heard and seen…" His dad gestured up the road. "I'm starting to wonder if I need to be worried."

Gabriel just shook his head, resting his hand on the window he needed to carry in, feeling his dad's gaze lingering on him. "Don't start," he said. "I'm fine, and you forget I'm a big boy. I can take care of myself…but since you're here, why don't you give me a hand bringing in this new window?"

His dad glanced at the window and at him. "I know you're a big boy…"

Gabriel let out a groan. His dad was one to never let anything drop.

"Hey, listen up," Andy said. "As your parents, we get to worry, we get to say something, but at the same time, it's your life you get to live. If I feel you're letting a pretty face steer you down a road to disaster, though, I will step in." His dad rested his hand on his shoulder again. "That's kind of a thing that happens. I love you, we love you. You got it?" There it was, the fear he had seen a time or two in his dad's eyes, that fatherly love, when he'd been so sick.

"Fine, I got it," he snapped, and this time his dad gave a soft chuckle and rustled his hair.

"Good, now I'll help you with this window—and one more thing."

He waited for it.

"We'll expect you to show up at the ranch for dinner tomorrow. I'll tell your mother you're coming, and then she can see for herself that you're okay."

Instead of answering, Gabriel pulled the window out. His dad grabbed the other end, and they lifted it off and out of the back of the truck.

Chapter Thirteen

She never cried.

Ever.

Not since she was eight, when her best friend at school had traded her up for the popular girls and proceeded to make her feel as if she was inadequate and unworthy of friendship. That had been the last time she'd ever shed a tear, until today. She was nestled in a corner of the comfy brown sofa, stuffing her face with potato chips, crumbs everywhere.

After MM's humiliating display at Moto Auto Parts, Barry had told her to take the rest of the day off—for her dignity or his, she wasn't sure. Nevertheless, after MM left, so had she, grabbing her purse, tucking it under her arm, and fleeing the store red-faced. She'd stopped at the corner store and grabbed a jumbo bag of salt and vinegar potato chips on sale, then walked home to eat her heart out and try to regain her dignity before she had to get up and go pick up Shaunty at preschool.

She sniffed and shoved another handful in her mouth,

reliving the horror of her morning, her cheeks puffed out and the skin on her face feeling raw from the tears that had streamed down for what felt like hours. Wads of toilet paper were all around her from blowing her nose. Crumbs covered her light T-shirt and jeans.

Just then, the front door opened, and there was Gabriel, carrying something long and heavy with a tall dark-haired man who was older and damn attractive. She didn't know what to do as she froze mid-chew and sat up straight, and they both took her in, shock on their faces.

It was in that moment, where no one said anything, that she wished the floor would open and swallow her up and put her out of her misery.

"Hey, I didn't know you were home," Gabriel, always the gentleman, said as she watched him put what she now saw was a window down. The other guy kicked the door closed with his foot and helped Gabriel lean the window against the wall.

She tried to chew faster and swallow the mouthful of chips without choking, and, with all the dignity she could muster, she brushed off the crumbs that covered her shirt front and piled up the wads of toilet paper on the sofa. Then she wiped her hand over her face to wipe off all the crumbs she knew had to be plastered there. This was worse than anything, she thought as she continued to sweep her hand over herself. She folded the bag of chips and put her bare feet on the floor, wanting to race down the hall to her room and hide, but she couldn't, because then she'd have to go past Gabriel and the very intense handsome man standing with him, who oozed a kind of power and confidence she didn't remember ever experiencing before. The expression on the man's face had her wishing this nightmare could end.

She looked over to Gabriel and had to sniff again, and she could see the moment they realized she'd been sitting there bawling like a baby. "Is everything okay?" Gabriel said and stepped closer to her even though he was still an arm's length away. She could hear the other man drag his hand over his face, the whiskers scraping. Obviously, he didn't have a clue what to say to a woman who had been sobbing, drowning herself in potato chips. She most likely appeared a train wreck.

"Oh, sorry, I'm so sorry," she said, not knowing what else to say. "I didn't know you'd be home so soon. I just was…" She couldn't figure out how to piece together a coherent sentence.

"Yeah, I, uh…I picked up the new window and was going to put it in. This is my dad, Andy." He gestured behind him, and she took in the man, who stepped in closer. "Dad, this is Elizabeth, who I was telling you about."

He actually held his hand out to her, and she turned hers over to see whether it was clean and then quickly gave it a wipe on her jeans, seeing the salt and chip bits still there. "So sorry about this mess." She stuck her hand in his large warm grip and took in his icy blue eyes. She wished she could find a way to excuse herself and leave the room. "It's nice to meet you." She pulled her hand away.

He nodded in silence and stepped in closer, taking in the room, the kitchen, and then her again. It was fricking unnerving.

"Sorry," she said again. By his face, his expression, Gabriel had definitely realized she'd been crying.

"You okay? You don't look okay." He gestured to her, and she wished he wouldn't. In fact, she wished he'd ignore it, because that was the right thing to do.

"Elizabeth, is it?" Andy said. "My son was telling me you have a daughter."

Thank God his dad got it and changed the subject, but then, as she stared at the man, she struggled to come up with something intelligent to say. "Yes, sorry, I didn't mean for…" She had to take a breath, because the way they were staring at her, they had to believe she was losing it. "I had a bad day. Doesn't happen often, and it just got the best of me, I'm babbling again, sorry. I do that when I'm nervous." She lifted the bag of chips she clutched in her hand and then folded it over, trying to pull herself together.

"Elizabeth has a sweet little girl, Shaunty. She's four," Gabriel said to his dad as he looked around and frowned. "Where is she?"

"Preschool until three. I should start walking down there to pick her up." She tapped her wrist out of habit where a watch would be if she actually owned a working one, wanting to find a way to make a polite exit, but neither Gabriel nor his father were moving or looking away.

"No, you don't have to walk," Gabriel said. "Seriously, I'll drive you. You don't need to rush and run out." He took a breath and crossed his arms, doing that gentlemanly thing again, except this was exactly the wrong time to be pulling that. "So was there a problem at work, something happen?" Why was he still asking her about it? He was supposed to pretend everything was fine.

"It was just MM showing up and causing a scene," she said. He had embarrassed the shit out of her. How could he have lied the way he did? That was why she'd cried and tucked herself onto the sofa in a ball, stuffing her face, trying to eat her way out of her misery. She took in the exchange between father and son.

"Damn him already," Gabriel said. "The sheriff said he was going to have a talk with him."

Elizabeth groaned, reaching down and grabbing the pile of toilet paper wads, and she walked over to the kitchen and put the bag of chips on the island, then dumped the used toilet paper into the garbage and wiped her hands on her jeans, again brushing off more of the salty crumbs. "He did, but look what happened," she said. "Should teach me that falling in love is for fools."

She hadn't meant to sound so jaded, but she was so tired of MM's shenanigans and feeling as if she couldn't get anything in her life to go right. "It's like I'll never be rid of him. Did you know he showed up today under the delusion that he could buy an engagement ring and propose and show me that he'd tattooed my name across his stomach, and I would love it and come back to him? When I saw what he'd done and was doing, I knew he wasn't getting the message I very clearly laid out, or so I thought. It's been almost two years since I left and walked out, and he won't take no for an answer. So today I was very, very clear that I won't…" She stopped talking, realizing she was venting at two men, Gabriel and his father, who she didn't know, giving them her heavy drama and personal history, and that was something she never did. Even her family didn't know all her escapades with MM and what she'd put up with, because she didn't want anyone to tell her what a stupid, idiotic fool she was.

"So this MM is the man who tried to take a round out of my son?" Andy said. "It's starting to sound like he's a little unstable. This is likely something you should get taken care of, see a lawyer and get a restraining order."

She wondered whether his father understood what he was saying. Likely not, by the looks of him. Some just never understood the obstacles others faced. Her priority was feeding and keeping a roof over her and her daughter's heads. Could she go back to her parents, Ruby and whatever guy she was hooked up with, for a period of time? Sure, if she wanted to lose her mind.

"Before I forget, Marty stopped by," Gabriel said. "We didn't realize you were home, and he asked me to give this to you." He handed her an envelope, and she took it and looked at the cash in it, mostly fives, tens, ones, but it was a lot to her. "He did say he planned on having a talk with MM, right before he also said how MM has put someone in the hospital."

She wasn't sure what to say about that. Yeah, that was one of the reasons she'd left him. Whatever it was that had gone on between him and some guy he worked with at the shipping yard, MM had beaten him pretty bad, broken his ribs, his nose, his jaw, and his eyes had been so swollen that he couldn't see. The guy hadn't pressed charges. "That was really kind of Marty," she said. "He shouldn't have, though." She rested the envelope on the counter with the chips and pulled in another breath. "Marty shouldn't be involving himself in this. He could get hurt."

All of a sudden, Gabriel's face took on an expression that almost bordered on annoyance, she thought, or maybe it was disbelief. His dad walked around the island and leaned against the sink behind her as if he needed to take this in from a distance. It was really unnerving, the way he kept watching her as if he could read her and knew everything she was thinking and feeling.

"You know what, Elizabeth?" Gabriel said. "Yes, your brother should say something to this guy. Somebody has to. Somebody needs to help MM figure out clearly that what he's doing isn't healthy for him, and maybe your brother is exactly the kind of guy to do it, bring in some of his biker friends and really teach him a lesson, lean on him and scare the ever-living crap out of him, because sometimes that's the only thing someone like MM will understand."

What the hell was he talking about?

"Maybe having a gang of some badass bikers putting the fear of God into him is exactly what he needs to walk away and leave you alone forever," Gabriel actually snapped.

She had to look over to his father, who wasn't saying a word, and she couldn't help wondering what he had to be thinking. "I'm not sure what you think Marty can do," she started, "but I can honestly tell you that if he goes over to MM's, he's likely to end up hurt. You seem to be under some impression that my brother is…" She crossed her arms and took a step to Gabriel, seeing the confusion on his face.

"A biker, part of a gang," he said and gestured as if she needed help understanding.

She wanted to laugh. People assumed a lot of things that weren't true. "Marty is one of the sweetest guys you'll ever know," she said. "He's not part of a bike gang and never has been. Yes, he loves his Harley, which is his baby, but that's it. What would have given you the impression he's some badass biker? I guess I'm dying to know!" She had to fight the urge to laugh.

The look on Gabriel's face was priceless. "Oh, the tattoos that cover his entire arm, the way he dresses as if he's part of a gang, the whole biker outfit, the way he stares you down and carries himself, the chain in his pocket that's attached to…what? So I just assumed—"

"Well, you assumed wrong, and tattoos have nothing to do with being a biker. I guarantee you more than half the population of the world, if not more, has at least one tattoo. It's art to Marty and a way for him to express himself. When he was fourteen, he got the crap beaten out of him by a couple of thugs in school and went down a dark path, with smoking, drinking, drugs, but he's cleaned it up except for the cigarettes, which he's never shaken. The chain in his pocket is linked to a watch from my grandfather. He wears what he does because it gives him confidence, but make no mistake, Marty is a sweetheart who wouldn't hurt a fly and is the most dependable person I know." She pressed both her hands to her face before pulling them away. "I should call him, and I need to go and get Shaunty."

Gabriel was now frowning and looking over to his dad. "Really, he's not a biker, part of a gang?" It was as if he didn't believe her, and he lifted his hands.

She shook her head. "No and no."

"Well, then…my bad. I'm sorry, really, I am. I don't even know what to say."

She stepped over to Gabriel and rested her hand on his shoulder to stop him. "It's fine. Now, you know, I really need to go and get Shaunty. You stay here and put that window in." She let her hand fall away and gave her shirt another sweep.

"Yeah, son," Andy said. "Put the window in, and I'll give Elizabeth here a ride."

She took in his father, who was striding her way and past her to the door, which he pulled open. "Ready?" he said to her as if it was decided, as if he had no intention of taking no for an answer, so she slipped her sandals on, having to look up at what a big man he was, trying to see the resemblance to Gabriel. She couldn't.

"And don't forget you're coming for dinner tomorrow," Andy said to Gabriel as they stepped past him out the door.

"Yeah, I know," he said, but when he glanced her way, his expression was filled with something that left her completely unsettled. This wasn't good, because that look was one of a man whose interest was crossing the line, not keeping everything on an impersonal level.

Been there, done that—and that was something she couldn't have.

Chapter Fourteen

Andy actually opened the door for her, just like his son had. Now she knew where the gentlemanly gestures that seemed to be a part of Gabriel came from, except, unlike Gabriel, Andy said very little. At the same time, everything about him was unnerving. Did he like her? Did he hate her? She was uncomfortable with the man whose extremely nice truck she was sitting in.

Andy shoved a key in the ignition, and she rested her hands on the leather of the passenger seat. She couldn't remember if she'd ever been in a vehicle this nice. He glanced her way only after he'd slid on sunglasses and started the truck, and she didn't miss how he took in her seatbelt without saying a word, she assumed to make sure she had it on.

"Well, thank you for driving me, but you didn't have to. I could have walked. It's a nice walk."

He made a face, and she thought it was amusement, but he said nothing as he pulled out and looked to her. "Which way?" he asked, and she just lifted her hand and pointed.

"It's over by the mall, actually just before it." She pursed her lips and glanced out the passenger window, at a loss for how to make small talk, considering he wasn't responding to her ridiculous babble anyway. How long would it take to get there? Five to ten minutes—no, maybe eight, depending on how fast he drove. She glanced to the clock and realized he was staring straight ahead, chewing gum, and he seemed so focused and intent on what he was doing. A deep thinker, nothing like Gabriel.

"So where exactly do you work?" He didn't look her way.

"Moto Auto Parts." She gestured out the window as if he could see the direction she was pointing, another nervous habit of hers. She finally fisted her hands and pulled them into her lap. She was sitting ramrod straight, feeling gritty and salty and wanting nothing more than to go home and have a bath. Later, after Shaunty was in bed.

"That's Barry Ogilvie's place, right?"

Oh no! She wanted to crawl in a hole and bury her head, because knowing Barry would mean Andy would likely hear everything about her, everything about her humiliating scene that day.

"Yeah, one and the same," she said, feeling the pinch in her jaw as she ground down on it harder than normal. She willed the light they stopped at to turn and get her to the preschool faster, where he could drop her off and hopefully never see her again.

"He's in kind of a financial bind right now," Andy said. "I heard he's barely making it and is only one step from shutting his doors." The way he said it, she wasn't sure if it was a question or a statement, and then he glanced her way. "That's a pretty unstable position for a single mom like you."

She didn't have a clue what she was supposed to say to

that. "Well, not a lot of options." The only type of work she was qualified for was entry level, and most places hiring offered barely above minimum wage. This was just a long line of things she'd never figured out, including what she really wanted to do.

"I suppose that's true," he said, and she just stared over at him as he drove, not sure what to add. He glanced her way again. "Ever thought about waitressing? Heard tips can be pretty good."

She wondered what he meant by that, and she had to stop herself from jumping straight to taking it the wrong way, which she was starting to do. "Like a bar, a night-club?" She could feel the way he looked at her as she spotted the corner house before the mall. "Right there is the daycare. You can just pull up and drop me off…" She lifted her hand, ready to jump up and down with relief over the fact that she could get out of the truck and out from the scrutiny she felt herself pinned under.

He drove right past the building to the small parking lot at the side and pulled into a stall before putting the truck in park, turning off the ignition, and opening his door. What was he doing?

"You know what? Thank you, Mister Friessen, for the ride, but I can walk back with Shaunty."

After he'd stepped out of the vehicle, he leaned in and lifted his shades, taking her in as if he'd decided something. "No, I'll drive you back, you and your girl." Then he glanced away for a second before turning his gaze back on her, and she could feel the way her stomach bottomed out at the way he looked at her. "And just to be clear, I certainly am not talking about a nightclub. I'm talking about a restaurant, a place where you can get some good tips. It was just a suggestion."

He gestured for her to get out, and she felt like an idiot.

She walked around the front of the truck, where he was standing, waiting for her, and she pulled in a breath to say something but couldn't think of anything, so she walked past him to the front door. He fell in beside her, and she had to glance over and up to him, and she still didn't have a clue what to say. He seemed to be taking in everything in a way that was so unnerving. At the same time, she was sure he wasn't accompanying her out of the goodness of his heart.

She walked into the daycare, seeing Shaunty with six other kids, sitting on a long bench, putting on her shoes. She lifted her hand to the owner, Betty, an older graying woman with thick glasses, then reached for Shaunty's hand without saying a word.

"Mommy, who's this?" Shaunty asked as she ushered her out the door. Andy closed it behind them.

"This is Gabriel's dad. He drove me here to pick you up, and now you get to have a ride home in a really nice truck." She made herself stop talking, because now she was sounding ridiculous, the way she was babbling on to her daughter, who pulled her hand from hers and looked up and over at Andy.

"You're Gabriel's father? You know he made me and Mom dinner? It was really good, fish. I've never had fish before."

The way Andy was watching her daughter, she noted the hint of amusement that touched the sides of his lips. "So then you know what a good cook he is," Andy said. "Didn't get it from me, though." He pulled open the back door. "Come on over here, Shaunty. You get to have the entire back seat to yourself." Then he lifted her daughter in, and Elizabeth hesitated only a second before walking around to the passenger side. She really was not used to someone taking over like this with her daughter, with her, and she was starting to see a lot of Gabriel's personality and qualities and where he'd gotten them from.

"So who taught Gabriel to cook if you didn't?" Shaunty asked.

Andy slid behind the wheel and fastened his belt, and she noticed he now had a softness about him as he glanced in the rearview mirror to her daughter. So he liked kids. "My wife, Gabriel's mother, a good woman who looks after us and keeps us fed and everything else, kind of how your mom looks after you," he said. For a second, she wondered if there was a hidden meaning in his words.

"Mom and me are being really frugal right now. Do you ever have to be frugal?"

"Shaunty," she said, jumping in before her daughter could say anything else to embarrass her. "You know you don't need to share everything." She glanced over her shoulder, staring at her. Shaunty was sitting in the back seat, not getting that there were some things you didn't talk about. Elizabeth hoped she was figuring it out by the way she narrowed her gaze at her.

"You know what, Shaunty?" Andy said. "I've never had to be frugal. I grew up with more than enough, more than I needed, in a big house, and I never knew what it was like to have less, like you and your mom, but that was how I met my wife and Gabriel."

She turned sharply to stare at him. "You're not Gabriel's father?" She couldn't stop herself from blurting it out, and this time Shaunty said nothing.

"I am his father. A father is someone who loves his kids, who's there for his son. That's what a father is. Any fool can father a child, but very few can actually be a father to a child." He lowered his voice as he said it to her, and she didn't know what to say. MM loved Shaunty in his own way, but he didn't have a clue how to be a father, or how to be in a relationship, or how to have any idea of what responsibility meant.

As she rode the rest of the way in silence, she listened to the back-and-forth chatter of this man, Gabriel's father, with her child, and he seemed so comfortable talking to Shaunty, a different man than the one who'd driven her before. If this was how he'd been with Gabriel, she could see now how lucky he was.

Chapter Fifteen

Elizabeth had been on the phone since walking through the door with Shaunty after his dad had dropped them off—talking with her mother, Gabriel thought, from the side of the conversation he could pick up. She was talking about how Marty was thinking it would be a good idea to confront her ex.

Gabriel had installed the window, stuck in the shims, and sealed it up. "So how was school?" he asked Shaunty, the precocious four-year-old, as she sat on a stool at the island, ready to share her day with him.

"It's called preschool, and it was good, except there was some man who came today and told Mrs. Perkins that the tire swings in back have to go. She was arguing with him about it, and she told us he's a government guy who likes to go around ruining fun for kids."

Gabriel had to smile. For a minute, he wasn't sure what she was getting at, but then he realized all the new safety policies they kept implementing. Some people thought kids could get hurt on just about everything. "Right, I think it's a safety thing. They're afraid of kids getting hurt, you know, liability."

She frowned, and he had to laugh. "Huh," she said. Yeah, she didn't get it, and neither did he, so he reached over and ruffled her out-of-control kinky hair. She was just one of those kids that he realized could sneak into his heart when he wasn't paying attention.

"It's a thing adults say because they're worried of something bad happening. You're right, it is silly." It was as if everyone had forgotten about taking responsibility for themselves and was too busy looking to blame everyone else for everything, looking at what could go wrong instead of living. "So, dinner, how about steak and grilled vegetables, asparagus, carrots? I'll whip up a béarnaise sauce to go with."

She made a face. "I thought Mom said tuna sandwiches tonight."

He took the little girl in just as her mom walked into the kitchen. He pulled two steaks out of the fridge and rested them on the counter.

"Right, dinner," Elizabeth said. She squeezed her hands together and gestured to Shaunty.

"Gabriel said we're having steak with…what did you say we were having again? Bear sauce?" She was so patient and the kind of kid that was fun to have around. She had already slipped into his heart to steal a little piece of it.

"Béarnaise," he said. "It's French, delicious, and you'll like it." He couldn't help the easy smile that touched his lips.

"Can I talk to you a second?" Elizabeth said, and he glanced over to her. She was staring daggers his way, and he was at a loss as to what he'd done. "Shaunty, why don't you go play with your dolls in our room or pull out your coloring book until dinner is ready?"

He took in Shaunty, who looked from him to her mom and then slid off the stool. "Mom, if you want to have alone time and adult talk with Gabriel, you just have to say so."

Holy crap, he couldn't believe she'd said that!

Elizabeth quirked a brow. "I want to have adult talk with Gabriel without you overhearing, so you, little miss, go play in our bedroom."

He noticed the way she pointed down the hall and then waited until Shaunty was out of the room, then crossed her arms under her amazing breasts. He couldn't get the image out of his mind of walking in on her with his dad, her face tearstained and red as she shoved potato chips in her mouth. He knew she was embarrassed, and he would have done anything to take away her pain, seeing how vulnerable she was. Then she turned back to him.

"Although I appreciate you cooking us dinner the first night, you cannot again. We are not eating your food. You are not feeding us. We're not a charity case. I have a perfectly good can of tuna and mayonnaise—oh, and before I forget, I also owe you money for the groceries." She reached into the envelope of cash that was still on the counter and pulled out bills, counting them, then extended a handful to him.

For a second, he just stared back at her, knowing he should take it, but at the same time, it was just one more thing he'd be taking from her when he knew she had nothing. He crossed his arms over his chest, walking around the island, which he noticed she had kept as an obstacle between them, until he stood right in front of her.

"I told you before, wait until your payday. It's not a big deal, and you're trying to tell me that opening a can of tuna and making a sandwich is better than steak? I think not," he said and took in the way her jaw slackened.

"Gabriel, of course it's not better. That's not the point. The point is you can't be cooking for us." She was still holding the bills.

There it was, these boundaries she kept erecting. Logically, if he really thought about it, that kind of went with the territory of having a roommate, except there was something about Elizabeth that made him want to look after her. He wanted to knock down every single barrier she'd put up to keep him and everyone else out. It was crazy, and if he said anything to anyone he knew, they'd say he'd lost his mind.

"Why not?" he said, trying not to smile from the fire that had started to sizzle between them. It was in her personality and the energy between them every time they were together in a room. She stirred something in him, and he had to fight the want, the need, to change things in the dynamic of their relationship. He had never felt this way about a woman before, and he knew she had to feel it too, but by the expression on her face, he thought for a second that she might deck him.

"Why not? You seriously asked me why not, Gabriel? I pay you rent to live here. You can't cook for me and Shaunty, feeding us. That's crossing way too many boundaries. We share a kitchen, but my food is over there in that cupboard. Although it isn't on the same level of quality as what you cook, it's still food, and…"

"You cook tomorrow night," he said, interrupting her. For a minute, she just gaped as if he'd pulled the rug out from under her, and she stared for another second before she blinked, pulled in a breath, and took a step back. She gestured around the kitchen but said nothing for another second.

"You want me to cook tomorrow for us, all of us," she said.

He shrugged. "No sense both of us cooking every night. I'll cook tonight, you tomorrow, and we'll switch—and besides, the steaks are thawed and ready…"

She held up the flat of her hand, and he could see she was having trouble trying to put two words together, appearing rattled, which was also something he didn't think happened to Elizabeth often. "Wait, let me get this straight. You want me to cook for you with my food when I know how healthy you eat? I somehow don't think you're up to bargain store mac and cheese, or a ground beef surprise casserole, or…"

He reached over and touched her hand, which was still holding the cash, and rubbed it gently, feeling the heat from her reaction. Then he pulled his hand away. "You're right. I won't eat that, but you shouldn't either. Steak tonight, tomorrow something else, and we'll work out a new arrangement."

He didn't have to touch her to see how she stiffened. She had taken it the wrong way, so he quickly added, "The arrangement of you and me sharing the cooking and deciding together on what we're going to have. That's what I mean." *Good recovery.* He wanted to pat himself on the back, but she frowned.

"Gabriel, I've seen what you eat, and there's no way I can afford that…" she started.

He could see she was getting ready to argue, so he reached out and touched her hand again. "We'll work it out, but I'm starving. How about let's just table this for now, and I'll make dinner. You had a tough day. Why don't you go have a bath before we eat?"

She was still frowning. "I'm not sure about this, Gabriel." She stared down at the money in her hand, and he gently touched it again.

"Well, I am. It's just dinner. Go have a bath, and after dinner we'll talk and figure it out."

She just stared at him for a second, and he could see the way she was thinking.

"Come on," he said. "Go, go. You have a bath, and Shaunty can help me with dinner."

"I still don't agree with this and can only see how you're the one getting the short end of the stick." She held up the cash again to him, but he shook his head.

"No, keep it. Next payday, I already said."

She shook her head and tucked the bills back into the envelope, then looked around the kitchen again before her gorgeous dark eyes landed back on him. He saw it then, a raw vulnerability, and he could see she was starting to think, which wasn't a good thing.

"So you talked to Marty," he said. "I know you didn't want him going over to see MM."

Great, change the subject.

She shrugged and actually slid out a stool and sat down, so he walked around the counter and pulled out a cookie sheet before unwrapping the steaks.

"He wouldn't answer his phone, but he does that when he has his music on. I talked to my mom and Ruby, and Ruby said she was going over to see him anyway and would have a talk with him about staying far away from MM. Not that he'll listen, mind you, but then, I wouldn't put it past Ruby to tag along with him and, between the two of them, do something really stupid."

He sprinkled salt and pepper onto the meat, both sides, and then washed his hands at the sink, seeing how she was worrying her lip, thinking. He couldn't help wondering how her family had created her, considering, to him, she was like perfection. "You said MM came into your work and embarrassed you. What did he say?"

She actually shut her eyes, glanced to the ceiling, and groaned as he pulled out carrots and asparagus from the fridge. He rested them on the counter and put a heavy cast-iron frying pan on the gas stove, then turned on the flame to heat it up.

"He lied," she said with sadness, the kind he'd never seen in her eyes before.

"What did he lie about? It was obviously something pretty bad to upset you like it did." He pulled butter from the fridge and dumped a hunk into the frying pan, then poured in olive oil. When he glanced back to Elizabeth, she was staring at her fingers, and he remembered how she'd looked earlier when he'd walked in with his dad.

"Other than causing a scene at work, demanding to see me, and being an asshole…" She lifted her gaze to him, and she seemed to again become the tough girl who wouldn't let anyone in. "He announced to everyone, after I spelled it out clearly how over we were, that I owed him."

He could see she was going to say more, and he waited, never pulling his gaze from hers as she stared at him with dark eyes, the eyes of a girl who'd had the shit kicked out of her one too many times. "For what, Elizabeth? He said you owed him for what?"

She touched her head, covering her eyes, and he could now see her embarrassment. She pulled her hand away. "He announced to everyone how I owe him because I forced him to get a vasectomy so he wouldn't knock me up again."

He wasn't sure what to say. He stared, and she gestured behind him to the stove.

"Your pan is smoking," she said.

He turned off the burner and then turned back to her, wondering why some idiot would get off on announcing something so personal to everyone. "I don't know what to say." He gestured toward her, watching as she folded her hands together.

"He lied, though," she said again.

"About…?" he started.

She rolled her eyes. "All of it. If he had a vasectomy, that was the first I heard about it. The fact is he got me pregnant by swapping out my birth control pills with a placebo. I can't even fathom how he did it, but he did, and he got me pregnant with Shaunty because I was going to leave him. It was his pathetic last-ditch effort to keep me, and he laughed about it. So there. Now you know my sordid, embarrassing history." She glanced over her shoulder, and he was at a loss for what to say. He watched her slide off the bar stool and reach for the envelope of cash. "And you know what? I think I will go and take that bath. Thanks for listening," she said.

This time, when she lifted her gaze to his, he could see her tough exterior crumbling a bit, giving him a glimpse into the vulnerable woman she was. She started out of the kitchen.

"Elizabeth," he said, and she turned her head but didn't look right at him. "Just for the record, that was a really shitty thing for him to do. I'm sorry."

He didn't know why he apologized, but he felt the need to say it on behalf of all males who weren't shitheads. He wasn't sure what she was thinking, but then she looked away and started down the hall, and he listened to her saying something to her daughter. Then he realized that she'd just trusted him with something he thought she likely hadn't shared with anyone else. Maybe he was getting somewhere after all.

Chapter Sixteen

She'd filled out five applications at pizza shops, family restaurants, and hardware stores, and she'd even talked to a temp agency about options in the area, but since she couldn't type and had no office or kitchen experience, no knowledge of computers or anything administrative or corporate, she was limited to service work, which again would be minimum wage, with crappy hours.

She was digging herself deeper into a life that was going nowhere. Oh, hindsight. If she could only go back… Back to what, though? She still didn't have a clue what she wanted to do. The only thing great about her life was the fact that she had the most incredible kid a parent could ever want and a few free hours in this comfortable house of Gabriel's until she had to pick up Shaunty. She stared at the cordless phone on the counter in the kitchen, willing it to ring. She'd left how many messages for Marty? And then Ruby too, but her cellphone kept going to voicemail.

She could call her mom, but then, she didn't feel like being stuck on the phone for an hour while her mother went on and on about the latest shenanigans of the neighbors, her dad, her sister's flavor of the week, or someone else her mother had cornered and questioned. So she instead pulled open the fridge and took in the package of ground beef, which was hers, and the fresh vegetables, which belonged to Gabriel, trying to figure out what she was going to cook tonight after that incredibly tasty and delicious steak he'd cooked for her and Shaunty the night before. She knew there was no way this could work.

The phone rang, and she shoved the fridge door closed. "Hey, Marty! Was wondering when you'd—"

"Elizabeth, it's Gabriel," he said, cutting her off. She could hear pounding in the background from the construction site where Gabriel worked.

"Oh, hi." Okay, that was weird. She wanted to cringe, but she was feeling embarrassed still about what she'd shared of her pathetic relationship with a man she still couldn't believe she'd fallen for.

"Yeah, listen, for dinner tonight, change of plans. Don't cook anything. We're going to my mom and dad's at the ranch."

She didn't know what to say, so she pulled the phone away and stared at the receiver. Right, hadn't his dad said something to Gabriel the night before in her moment of embarrassment about coming out for dinner?

"You mean you'll be having dinner? Shaunty and I will stay home." Tonight they'd have tuna, even though her daughter had made a point of telling Gabriel how much she'd loved his sauce and the vegetables, and she'd even asked for more steak.

He chuckled on the other end. "No, we'll all go—you, me, and Shaunty. My mom called, and she wants to meet you, and hey, you'll get to see where I grew up." He sounded happy.

She didn't think this was a good idea as she walked

through the empty house and down the hall to her bedroom, which was neat and tidy, with a new window and two air mattresses where she and her daughter had slept the night before. They were still inflated, and they looked like legless twin beds. "You know what? You go. That's your family, and I'm not sure…"

"Nonsense. I'll swing by and pick you up. I'll grab Shaunty first from preschool on my way home. She'll love it."

She actually stared at the phone again as she pulled the receiver away, because Gabriel wasn't hearing her. Of course her daughter would love it. She wouldn't, though, having to sit at a table with his parents, who were likely going to stare down their noses at her.

"Gabriel, seriously, no. I think it would be best if you go by yourself, and Shaunty and I will just stay here."

She could hear someone talking in the background.

"Listen, you're coming," he said. "My mom wants to meet you, and I've got to go. Give Shaunty's preschool a call and tell them I'll swing by and pick her up in about an hour. See ya." Then he hung up, and she just stared at the phone, wondering how he'd convinced her to go to his parents' for dinner when she'd basically said no.

What was it about Gabriel Friessen? She realized he could convince her into going along and doing things with him she'd sworn she'd never do. It was a dangerous road. She needed to sit him down and lay out the boundaries that he seemed to be crossing on a daily basis.

"Okay, as soon as he pulls up, you tell him that you and Shaunty are staying home, that he needs to go himself…even though him phoning was thoughtful." She stared in the bathroom mirror at her image, trying to shake off the fact that she'd never experienced this kind of thoughtfulness—cooking her dinner, calling her and telling her about dinner at his parents', even giving up his bed.

She pulled her hairbrush through her hair and took in her green and white sleeveless blouse, her loose jeans, and the hint of makeup she'd put on even though she was planning on staying home. She wanted to roll her eyes at herself, because she was feeling this tug of war inside, needing to keep her distance from a man she felt herself dangerously wanting to be around.

She heard the door and laughter.

"Hey, Elizabeth, you ready?" Gabriel called out, and she took in her daughter and Gabriel in his worn jeans covered in white sawdust from the construction site.

"Hi, Mom! Look what I made today." Her daughter had a wide smile and was carrying what looked like artwork, a mass of scribbles and globs of paint.

"Wow, that's amazing! You know what? This will look perfect on our bedroom wall, and hey, I was thinking that maybe we'd stay home tonight, just you and me, and…"

Her daughter was frowning, and she didn't have to look over to Gabriel to know that he was frowning too.

"But we can't, Mom. Gabriel is taking us to his family's ranch. He's also going to show me his horse. You did say that, right, Gabriel?"

Okay, now she wanted to kick him, and she wondered if he got it by the way she was staring at him, shooting daggers his way, or trying, her arms crossed. He glanced from her daughter to her.

"Of course I did," he said. "Listen, let me grab a quick shower and change. Elizabeth, seriously, this will be fun. You'll have fun. You'll like my family." He actually walked over to her, rested his hand on her shoulder, and stared down at her. Damn his eyes! She wasn't sure what the color was, a cross between green and blue, and he was so not

MM, but at the same time, she just didn't want this getting any more personal than it was.

"I'm sure I will, but, Gabriel, I've been thinking…"

"How about you just come?" He cut her off, his hand still resting on her shoulder. "Have dinner, and for once don't think about all the problems you think are going to happen or make this into something it isn't."

She didn't have a clue what to say as he glanced back to her daughter, who was still looking at her as if she were about to pull the rug out from under her. Damn, she had no choice.

"Fine," she said. "Shaunty, go put your picture in the kitchen for now." She reached for Gabriel's arm when he went to walk past her to his bedroom. "Can I talk to you a second?" She pulled him around the corner to his bedroom and stopped just outside his door, where her daughter couldn't see or hear them.

"Okay…?" He actually started to laugh and then stopped, likely from the expression on her face.

"Look, I know I said I would go, but, Gabriel, you can't be getting Shaunty's hopes up like that. We rent a room from you. Remember the boundaries thing? I can see she's starting to like you a lot, and now we're going to your parents' place for dinner …"

He grabbed her wrist, pulled her into his bedroom, and closed the door.

"Gabriel, what are you doing?"

"Getting you alone so I can talk to you without Shaunty hearing. You really have this thing about boundaries, and I get it. I'm starting to get a really clear picture of why you would put up all the walls you have, considering the guy you were involved with and the crap he continues to pull on you, but I'm not like that. Most guys aren't like that, and you know what? I'm starting to think this is more about you being scared." He was right in front of her and had her backed against the door now.

"I'm not scared. This isn't that," she said as she took in the hint of a smile that touched his lips.

"Oh yeah? Prove it."

What was he, two years old?

"I'm not proving it. Why would I do something like that? You're making this into something personal when our relationship is…"

He angled his head and then leaned in just a bit closer, his lips so close she could feel her heart jackhammering in her chest. She dipped her gaze to his lips, his full pink lips, and pressed back into the door, furious at herself for wishing that he'd just kiss her already. Then she shut her eyes and dug deep, pressing her hands to his chest, holding him back, and hating her hands for keeping all that hardness away from her.

"You should get in the shower," she bit out and then somehow slipped out of the bedroom.

"Elizabeth," he said.

She kept her back to him, two steps out and freezing. His voice was so deep and pulled in her stomach, and she was furious at the effect he was having. She said nothing.

"I'll be ready in five," he said, and then she heard him step up behind her and slip his finger over her shoulder, under her hair. She had to fight the shiver, wanting to lean back into his touch. "You just keep telling yourself this isn't personal, that something isn't happening between us," he said. "Except the only problem is your reaction to me tells me something else entirely. You're scared."

His warm breath had a shiver rising up all the way through her from her toes. Then he kissed her cheek so gently that her eyes shut, her breath caught, and he was gone.

She listened to his door close, and a second later, his shower turned on. "What are you doing, Elizabeth?" she said to herself, turning back to the closed door and envisioning the man who could draw her into a relationship she swore she would never be in again. No, it was time to definitely set some boundaries, some clear rules that were easy to follow and lines that wouldn't be crossed. The only problem was she'd have to make sure she first understood clearly what the rules were.

Chapter Seventeen

S he had never been west of the city, yet here she was in the passenger side of Gabriel's pickup, Shaunty between them, as he drove the highway.

Elizabeth had never been with a man who was a leader, an alpha, a man who took charge and made it seem as if that was part of who he was. Gabriel was driving them, caring for them, taking them to his parents' house, and it made her feel like a woman. With MM, it was always "I'll meet you there," or he'd be out all night without a word to her, or "Oops, won't be home. Don't wait up." Better yet, when he did walk back in in the morning, he always acted as if he'd done nothing wrong and didn't have to explain.

This with Gabriel was something she didn't understand, and she didn't know how to handle it. He treated her like a lady, a term she'd never really understood. As she sat quietly in the passenger side, only half listening to the back-and-forth between her daughter and Gabriel, it wasn't lost on her how good he was with Shaunty, and it wasn't that pretend interest people showed for kids.

"Do you know who your real dad is?" Shaunty said.

Elizabeth turned to her daughter, then to Gabriel. She wasn't sure what expression was on his face as he stared over the steering wheel and the open highway. "Shaunty, you shouldn't ask something like that," she said. "I'm sorry, Gabriel…"

He was shaking his head and glanced over to her, then down at Shaunty. "My real dad? Why would you ask that?"

For a minute, Elizabeth had a feeling he was embarrassed. "Uh, I think Shaunty means your biological father. When Andy gave me a lift to pick up Shaunty at daycare, he may have mentioned something about meeting you and your mom. He did add that a father is a man who raises a child, not fathers one," she added pointedly, giving her daughter a long, lingering look and hoping she would drop it.

What she didn't expect was the smile that touched Gabriel's lips. "Yeah, my dad was kind of my hero. I can still remember meeting him, being just a scared little kid. To answer your question, yeah, I know who my biological father is and what he did to my mom—got her pregnant at fifteen, turned his back on her, and left her to fend for herself. I can still remember the dumps we had to live in, being hungry." He shook his head. "That guy really isn't someone I want to know, even though he showed up when I was a kid, when I got childhood leukemia, to help. It was a nice thought, but it was my dad, Andy…" He glanced over to Shaunty and Elizabeth. "It was Andy who was there for me, has always been there for me, and he's my real father. He makes my mom really happy, and I think you two will really hit it off." He nudged Shaunty, and the way he smiled down at her daughter and the way her daughter giggled, Elizabeth was seeing another side of Gabriel that she didn't want to see. Damn him for being so fricking perfect!

"See up there, in the distance? That house is where we're going," Gabriel said. He was talking to her daughter again, and Elizabeth took in the ranch and the dusty gravel road. She could see horses, cattle, and land as far as the eye could see. Everything was open. Andy's dark pickup was parked in front along with a couple minivans and a few other cars. "You'll get to meet my brothers and sisters," Gabriel said, "and looks like a few others, too. That could be Blake and Brandyne…"

Elizabeth took in the men on the porch as she stopped listening, staring out the window at the three staring right at her. Her heart starting jackhammering, and she could feel a nervous sweat start under her arms. Andy held a beer and was talking with the other two, and no one was smiling. What was it about the way they were looking at her that gave her the feeling she wasn't exactly a wanted guest?

"So you're sure it's okay we're here?" she said. It sounded scared and pathetic to her own ears, and Gabriel turned off the truck and gave her an odd look.

"Of course. Come on, I'll introduce you to everyone." Then he was out his door.

Her daughter rested her hand on her arm, looking up to her. "Mom, it's okay. Don't be nervous."

Elizabeth didn't miss the way Gabriel was standing there, taking her in, really looking, and she didn't like the way it seemed as if he could see inside her and all of her vulnerabilities.

"Come on, Shaunty," Gabriel said and lifted out her daughter as Elizabeth pulled in a breath and made herself open the door and step out.

"Hey, Gabriel! It's about time you got here," said the man standing beside Andy.

Andy had an amused grin, she thought, but said

nothing as he watched her and then shifted his eyes in a second to her daughter, who'd come around the truck. She saw the moment his expression softened. Okay, so he had a soft spot for her daughter. Who didn't? She found herself moving over to her.

"Shaunty," she said and held out her hand, walking closer to the house. Her daughter's hand slipped into hers just as Gabriel's hands rested on her shoulders.

"Elizabeth, Shaunty, you've met my dad, but this is Blake, our sheriff," he said.

Blake stepped down from the top step, and the way he took her in, she couldn't help worry about what he was thinking and what he knew. He had dark hair and, like Andy, was also dangerously attractive. He held out his hand, and she was forced to let go of Shaunty's and shake it. He had a firm grip, and she could feel his eyes burning into her.

"Pleasure to meet you, Elizabeth…" He let it hang, and she knew he was waiting for her to tell him her family name. *Maybe for a record check!*

"Abercrombie," she said, pulling her hand from his and resting it around Shaunty again.

Andy gestured to her daughter, and what did she do but race up the stairs to him? He leaned down and said something to her that had a big smile plastered across her face as she replied, "Sure!"

Elizabeth was trying not to crane her neck, because she didn't have a clue what Andy had said. Then Andy pulled open the screen door and stepped into the house with her daughter, and Elizabeth lifted her hands, helpless over what to do.

"That other bum over there is my brother Jeremy," Gabriel said.

Elizabeth had to drag her gaze away from the door her

daughter and Andy had slipped through. Jeremy was maybe eighteen, nineteen, and the spitting image of his father. He had a brilliant smile, and she took in the blue eyes, different from Gabriel's. She was trying to see some of Gabriel in his brother and at the same time was feeling as if she were under a microscope from the sheriff.

"So you're Elizabeth," Jeremy said. "Great to meet you! Cute kid you got. Don't worry—my mom and dad will be spoiling her rotten. Wow, Dad wasn't kidding, Gabriel. She really is a looker."

Elizabeth wondered if this could get any more awkward. She heard the sheriff curse under his breath and chuckle before he took a swallow of his beer.

"Ignore my brother, please," Gabriel said. "There's a dark, twisted side of him that enjoys stirring things up and being an ass in general."

Jeremy stepped around the sheriff, laughing and holding out his hand. He was ripped, young, gorgeous, and she wished the ground would open up. "Apologies, Elizabeth. Welcome to our humble ranch."

Her hands were damp, and she actually unfisted one and gave it a wipe on her jeans before sticking it in his. "This is nice," she said. *Okay, that was a really original thing to say.* She turned her head to Gabriel as she pulled her hand from Jeremy's, and she could see the way he was shaking his head at his brother, the expression on his face far from amused.

"Where's Chelsea?" Gabriel asked, then turned to her. "Chelsea is one of my sisters, Jeremy's twin."

The screen door squeaked, and Andy stepped out, holding a platter of raw meat, steaks. He walked over to the barbecue she hadn't noticed.

"She flew out this morning with a friend to some resort place in Minnesota. Where was it again, Dad?"

Elizabeth felt Gabriel's hand on the small of her back now, urging her up the steps, where she stood awkwardly beside the sheriff, who wasn't saying anything, and Andy, who was now putting steaks on the grill.

"Bear Island," Andy said, then gestured with his tongs to Gabriel. "You and I need to have a chat about the cattle. We need to bring them in on Saturday. We've got a number of calves born and needing branding, and trucks coming to take eighty head into the slaughterhouse, so you need to be here at dawn. We're starting early." He then turned to Jeremy and said, "You get to help this weekend, too, along with Zachary and Sarah."

She was wondering who Zachary and Sarah were when she realized that they had to be his other brothers and sisters. Maybe she should have gotten a refresher from her mom, who had pried a bunch of personal information from Gabriel, before coming out so she would know who all the players were.

"Yeah, yeah, I got it," Gabriel said. "Listen, Elizabeth, do you want something to drink?"

"Ah, you know, it's okay…" Now they were all staring at her as if she'd said the most ridiculous thing. "Whatever you're having will be fine," she quickly added, and then he was gone into the house. His brother followed, and she was left with the sheriff and Andy, who weren't the least bit chatty.

"So heard you had some more trouble with that feller you were involved with," Blake said, staring down at her, his gaze intense, hard, and so fricking intimidating. Of course Andy, or was it Gabriel, had told him about MM's visit. How much did he know?

She shrugged. "He did, but I made it very clear this time we're done and not to bother me." *There, drop it. Let's move on.*

"Did you see a lawyer yet and get a restraining order on him? If he's harassing you now at work, you're going to have grounds."

The screen door popped open again, and Gabriel stepped out with a glass of ice water and a bottle of beer. Her eyes went right to him. He handed her the bottle.

"Kind of wanted to talk to you about that, Dad," he said, obviously having overheard. "Your lawyer…"

Elizabeth took the beer and wished she could be anywhere but there. Didn't they get it? She didn't have dollars to toss to some lawyer.

"Marlene Abelman. You call her?" Andy said.

Elizabeth wasn't sure what she saw in the exchange between father and son, so she lifted her beer and took a swallow.

"Was going to get Elizabeth in there for a sit-down so she can find out her options."

"Right, for a free consult," Elizabeth said before this could go any further and she had committed to something she couldn't possibly afford. "There won't be anything happening after that. Told you my funds are limited. My priority is my daughter."

"As she should be, but Marlene will still give you some help," Andy said. "Gabriel, give her a call first to make sure she sets aside time."

Elizabeth found herself glancing from father to son, feeling as if things were being taken care of and handled for her. She'd be told where to go, where to sit, and who to talk to. Then there was Blake, the sheriff, whose eyes she could still feel on her. She glanced over to him, and holy crap, he wasn't even smiling. It was as if he'd already figured out her pathetic history and was trying to judge what kind of trouble she was.

"You know, none of this may be necessary anyway,

since my brother is planning on going over and having a talk with him," she said. Now why would she say that? Maybe because she was hoping for them all to stop talking about it and acting as if they were going to step in and fix her problems.

"But if I recall correctly, you said your brother could end up getting hurt if he did." Gabriel was giving her everything in that intense gaze, the way his eyes appeared to darken. He shrugged, and of course he was waiting for her to say something.

"Hurt? Why would he get hurt?" the sheriff said. "Is there something I should know?"

Elizabeth stared at Gabriel, who didn't seem to get the fact that she wanted all this talk of her ex to die away so they could…what, have an uncomfortable dinner with people she didn't know?

"Yeah, uh, Elizabeth said MM had put someone in the hospital. Marty mentioned it too. Thought you were going to talk to your brother, put a stop to him going," Gabriel said.

Andy was watching her as she squeezed that bottle of beer with both hands.

"I left him a message," she said. "Talking to my sister, Ruby, too…"

The screen door squeaked. "Hey, did you say your last name was Abercrombie?" Jeremy poked his head out and looked at her.

"Uh, yeah."

He gestured into the house with his thumb. "Well, the news is on, and your daughter said something…"

"Mom! Mom!" Shaunty yelled, pushing out around Jeremy. "Uncle Marty and Aunt Ruby are on the news!"

"What? Why…?" She glanced up to Gabriel,

wondering if the horror she felt was reflected in the way she stared at him.

Jeremy was still holding the door open. "Some fight broke out at a bar, and three people were arrested," he said.

She opened her mouth to say something, but all that came out was air.

"Blake, maybe you can find out what's going on," Andy said.

The sheriff went in the house, and Elizabeth stared at Gabriel and his father. Her daughter was looking up at her, and the only thing she could say was, "I'm sorry."

Chapter Eighteen

"I'm so sorry," Elizabeth said again from the passenger seat of his pickup.

Gabriel knew she felt horrible, and this was at least the fourth time she'd apologized for what she perceived as ruining dinner. "Stop apologizing already," he said. "This isn't your fault. You're not responsible for any of this."

They were approaching the sheriff's office, where Blake would already be, since he'd left as soon as he saw the news. They'd learned that Marty, Ruby, and MM had all been arrested for the shitstorm they'd created at the Waddling Pig, a bar where not a week went by that the cops weren't called in.

"It is my fault, Gabriel. Seriously, whatever happened, Marty and Ruby were only there because of me, and now what must your parents think? I really don't think I should have left Shaunty with your mom." She wiped her hands over her face, and he could see how quickly she was heading to the point of thinking the worst.

"Elizabeth, first, Shaunty is better off with my mom at the ranch. You really think dragging her along to the jail is an ideal situation? My parents would never offer to watch her if they didn't mean it. Second, you don't know why they were arrested, no one does, which is why we're on our way there now. So take a breath."

She swept back the long dark waves of her hair, seeming rattled, before she nodded and worried her lip. "Okay, I get what you're saying, and you're right, of course. She's not better off being dragged to the jail, but I'm starting to feel as if I'm taking advantage of your parents, of you. Here you are now, driving me into town, when you should be at your parents', having dinner. This is my problem, not yours. This is just too much, Gabriel. And as far as my brother and sister are concerned, though I may not know the exact details, I do know they had every intention of tracking MM down for me and getting him to leave me alone and stop his unruly behavior."

He could hear the tension in her voice. When he glanced in his rearview mirror and saw his dad's pickup right behind him, he didn't think he should mention it to Elizabeth, considering how acute her embarrassment still was. They'd all gathered around the TV in the family room when it showed the recap of her sister, brother, and MM being led out of the bar handcuffed and stuck in the back of two cop cars. Their names had even flashed across the bottom of the screen.

"Elizabeth, it's not lost on me how you have a hard time asking for help. You need to stop apologizing. I'm not sure how many times I can say it to you. Of course I'm coming, and Blake is already there. He'll assess the situation, find out the real story, whatever that is, and then we can go from there. No point panicking until you know what the situation is. And for the record, mom loves kids, and Shaunty will have a great time with my brothers and sister."

Sarah was in her teenage years, at an age where she loved babysitting kids, and Zachary would ignore her, of course. Jeremy would probably have her idolizing him. Regardless, his mom had insisted that Shaunty stay, even though she hadn't had the chance to get to know Elizabeth other than a quick hi and bye as her siblings were being arrested and paraded out of a bar on live TV.

"Why are you doing this, Gabriel, being so helpful and a gentleman? You should just walk away, you know, because we barely know each other. Do you have some expectation of me? Because I just don't get it."

For a second, he didn't know what she meant as he pulled in front of the sheriff's station. Blake and Brandyne's minivan was parked out front, and he pulled in beside it. His dad parked his truck on the other side, and he took in the moment that Elizabeth spotted him and he shoved his truck in park and turned the key.

He wanted to reach out and shake her when the meaning of what she'd said sank in. "You know what, Elizabeth? You must have a pretty low opinion of me and men in general if you think I have some expectation of you. From how you said it, you must think me some kind of dog, that I'd…what, think you owe me something because I'm doing the right thing and—" He stopped talking before he could blurt out that he cared about her. Right about now, he didn't think she wanted to hear it, or maybe she couldn't hear it. "The thing is, Elizabeth, you're beating yourself up for something someone else is doing, and you're not responsible for the actions of your brother, your sister, or the guy you were involved with. The only person you're responsible for is you. So if you don't mind, how about we go in, find out the score? Then we'll table this little discussion for later and I can figure out why you seem to think I should just kick you to the curb." He knew it had come out sharper than expected, and with an edge of anger. Maybe that was why she pursed her lips, yanked her door open, and stepped out to where his dad was now standing, waiting. He said something to her that Gabriel couldn't make out.

By the time he went around the front of the truck, his dad was already walking up the six concrete steps, Elizabeth following behind him. Gabriel fell in beside her, seeing how tense she was. His dad held open the door for her, and he didn't have to say a word to Gabriel; his gaze said everything about how he too had picked up on Elizabeth's state of mind. Blake was behind the front desk in the bullpen of the office, talking with a deputy who'd spotted them. Another was on a phone at the back along with an older woman with graying hair.

"Come around," Blake said, waving them in. "Was just getting all the details of what happened." He handed a file to the officer, and Andy stepped through the gate and gestured for Elizabeth and Gabriel to follow. He took in the deputy now answering the phone as Blake led the way into his office. It was busy today, and he didn't spot anything that gave him any idea where Elizabeth's siblings and ex could be stashed.

"So where are my brother and sister?" Elizabeth asked as they stepped into the office.

Blake shut the door. Andy rested his hands on his hips and was watching Elizabeth, who was standing straight, her chin lifted. Gabriel was starting to see how she held everything so close to her to keep everyone from seeing her vulnerability. That tough exterior that was so damn independent was starting to crack.

"In lockup right now after a fight broke out at the bar. The owner called us in. Seems there was quite a disturbance—some chairs broken, glasses shattered..."

"Marty and Ruby did that?" Elizabeth interrupted. Gabriel could see the horror on her face and at the same time the annoyance on Blake's because she wasn't letting him finish.

"Elizabeth…" Gabriel said and rested his hand on her shoulder, which was so tense. He let his hand slide away when she lifted both of hers and tossed him an uneasy glance. He didn't miss the exchange between his dad and Blake.

"Not necessarily," Blake said. "It was a disagreement, I understand, with this ex of yours. The two confronted him over by the pool tables, and no one is saying who started what, but by the time my deputies got there, Ruby and Marty had MM pinned down, and they'd made quite a mess."

"You're telling me my sister and brother had MM on the ground and not the other way around?" Elizabeth started laughing, and he wasn't sure what to make of it.

"So are charges being filed against them?" Andy asked.

Elizabeth touched her forehead and then pulled her hand away as if she couldn't believe what she was hearing.

"Well, that's up to the owner of the bar, but see it from his point of view: He's tired of the fights and damage that keeps coming out of his pocket, even though that place has been a thorn in my side for years, and it attracts everyone bad. No surprise that the three of them are now barred from returning, considering the ongoing trouble there. From the witnesses, it sounds as if your brother and sister were the ones who started it." Blake settled his gaze on Elizabeth, while Andy dragged his hand over his chin and the whiskers there.

"I want to see them, Marty and Ruby, please. Are they hurt?" she said.

Blake didn't say anything for a minute as he stared at

her with his heavy gaze, the one Gabriel always felt uncomfortable under. "No, everyone seems to have escape unscathed, other than being sore tomorrow, some scraped knuckles, and likely a shiner for that ex of yours. I guess what's going through my mind is why? MM is volatile, yet your siblings go and start something? I don't like this kind of shit going down in my county, and there isn't a week that passes where my deputies aren't called to some disturbance at that bar."

Blake had his arms crossed, perched on the side of his desk, and Gabriel could feel how Elizabeth still believed this was all on her.

"You know what, Blake?" Gabriel said. "She's just asking to see her sister and brother, that's all. I know all too well what comes at you with the likes of MM, and although, as I said to Elizabeth, we don't know all the details, she's just asking to see them, to see if they're okay. I know they were concerned over MM's constant interference, turning Elizabeth's life upside down, showing up where she lives, where she works. They felt the need to do something, which is only right, because you know as well as I do…"

"Fine, I get it," Blake said. He gave a sharp nod and then walked around the desk to pick up his phone. "Can you bring the Abercrombies up?"

Andy angled his head, and Gabriel thought a hint of amusement touched his lips as he looked from him to Elizabeth.

"No, both of them," Blake said, then hung up the phone.

Elizabeth still hadn't said anything but was now staring down at her hands, fussing with them. Another nervous habit, he thought.

"You kind of didn't answer about charges for any of

them," Andy said, and the exchanged glance between him and Blake was unusual. "Because, you know, bringing them up here for a talk when I'm pretty sure they've been mirandized, and not having a lawyer…"

"I'd like to talk to my brother and sister alone," Elizabeth interrupted, lowering her hands. Her eyes seemed to flash with fury as if she'd figured out that her siblings could be in jeopardy with Blake around to listen.

There was a tap on the door. Then it popped open, a deputy in the doorway, and Gabriel spotted Ruby with a red mark on her face, her auburn tank ripped at the side. Marty was behind her and didn't appear to have a scratch on him until he saw his hands. His knuckles were scraped and red as the bruising started to set in. Neither looked happy.

Elizabeth lifted her chin and let her gaze land on the sheriff, Andy, and him. "Thank you, but I'd appreciate it if you'd all give us a moment to speak alone." She crossed her arms as if ready to stand her ground, and Gabriel took in Marty and Ruby, who were standing just inside the door.

Blake nodded to the deputies. "Fine, I'll give you a few moments," he said, and he started to the door and walked out. Andy followed and turned back to him.

"You know what? No," Gabriel said, looking straight at Elizabeth. "I'm staying."

Andy seemed to understand, because he closed the door, leaving Gabriel with Elizabeth and her siblings. Gabriel took in the odd exchange between Marty and Ruby and the fact that Elizabeth seemed far from happy.

Chapter Nineteen

Elizabeth hugged her sister. "Are you okay? Did he hurt you? Oh, Ruby, what were you thinking, going in there, going around him?"

"I'm fine. It was actually kind of fun, you know," Ruby said, but Elizabeth noticed she had winced and gripped her shoulder. She took a closer look, seeing the telltale signs of bruising. At the same time, she was rattled because Gabriel was refusing to leave. This wasn't okay, and she couldn't turn around and look at him.

"You're hurt! Seriously, did they bring a doctor in for you?"

Her sister was shaking her head and made a face. "No. Don't you worry none about that. I told you I'm fine, just a little sore, but I'll be fine by tomorrow."

Elizabeth glanced up to Marty, who was watching Gabriel. "Marty, what were you thinking? Why would you two start something with MM? You know how volatile he is. Did you go looking for him?"

She took in the way Marty shifted his gaze back to her

from Gabriel, and she could see the uncertainty, as if he was deciding on something.

"Hey, he's done enough, Lizzie, and you and that niece of mine are done having to move and run because he won't leave you be. You have a nice place now. Gabriel, it warms my heart to see you here with my sister." Marty actually gestured between them. It was a guy thing, she thought, but she couldn't look back to see how Gabriel responded. She stared in horror, taking in the way Marty gave Gabriel a nod as if they had talked and decided and were on the same page about her. So she turned to her sister.

"And you…I asked you to talk to Marty about staying away from MM, and here you are instead, doing what but tagging along with him and not keeping him away from trouble!"

Ruby laughed. "Funny thing about that. Marty here has been looking for MM for how long, and he wasn't at that dive of an apartment you shared with him, or at work, or any of the usual hangouts. It was kind of on a whim that we stopped in at the Waddling Pig…"

"And there he was," Marty finished. "This was after we had ordered a pitcher of draft to discuss how we can fix your life so you can move on with prince charming here."

She took in the way her sister smiled past her, and now she wished the floor would open up and swallow her. She wondered how wide her eyes were as she stared daggers at her sister. "Ruby, seriously…"

"And there he was, hanging with a couple of lowlifes around the pool table with a girl hanging off his arm, very much together, kissing and laughing, doing shots," Marty interrupted.

"He hasn't changed," Ruby said. "We just watched as he carried on, and we're like, it's time we have a talk to him and set him straight about messing with the Abercrombies. So I was the one who walked over there. Marty was still at the bar, watching, and MM didn't see me at first. I had to tap his shoulder while he was lip-locked to that mousy thing, with a huge rack that was stuffed in a tank two sizes too small, a ton of makeup, and didn't look like much for brains. He turned, giving me that asshole smile as if we were long-lost kin or something." Ruby picked at the tear in her shirt before crossing her arms.

"What is it about that flashy smile he uses on everyone, thinking it will get him anything he wants?" Marty said. "It's so phony, plastic. Sorry, Lizzie."

She couldn't help feeling as if he were reminding her how stupid she was. "Fine, I get it, the smile, and then what? Why the fight?" She fisted her hands at her sides, turning to see Gabriel leaning against the sheriff's desk, his arms crossed and watching her in a way that had her stomach doing a flip. How could he still not be walking out that door? He was still there, and she needed to wrap her head around the fact that her brother and sister were in some seriously deep shit all because of her.

"It was me, okay?" Ruby said. "I called him out about harassing you and not leaving you alone, wanting you back like a stalker, yet there he was hooked up with some babe in a bar, carrying on like a sleazy scumbag, and he laughed at me as he slid his arm around her, both of them far from sober, and he said he would decide when he was done with you, not you or anyone else. That chick just stayed there instead of realizing what a dog he was, and I suddenly just fisted my hand and popped him in the face." Ruby lifted her right hand, taking in the slight swell of her knuckles and grinning.

"Yeah, it was priceless," Marty said. "She nailed him, and he stumbled a bit and lost his balance, falling on the pool table. I think he was as shocked as everyone, as the guys he was with started laughing, kind of emasculating him, saying he could be taken down by a woman. When he got on his feet, it was like he couldn't believe Ruby would actually land a punch on him, right in his eye. I was standing there, thinking my sister is the first woman to get one over on him. Then next thing I knew, he hit her back, landed a punch right here." Marty gestured to Ruby's cheek, which was red, and she just shrugged.

"And that was it," she said. "Next I knew, Marty yelled and charged him and took him down over one of the tables and broke it, glasses and everything on it. I sort of got in on it, and then next I know the cops are there and cuffing us and hauling us out, and here you are." Ruby reached up and touched her lip. "You know that was the first time I was ever in the back of a cop car?"

Elizabeth looked back to Gabriel, who ran both hands over his face, and she thought for a second he'd realize this was all too much and walk out. This was it. Then he lowered his hands.

"Okay, you know what? I totally get it," he said. "Let me talk with Blake and see if we can't get this to go away. Maybe he can talk to the bar owner and convince him to let it go, pay for the damages, and everyone walks away. Let's not forget MM, either."

She could see the way he was considering something.

"I think that's a great idea," Marty said. "Geez, Lizzie, you picked a good one here." Her brother gestured to him, and the grin on his face was priceless, as was her shock when she realized what he'd said.

"Whoa there, Marty, you're confused," she said. "I'm renting a room from Gabriel. That's all."

And he'd taken her to his parents' for a dinner that they hadn't had because her brother and sister had decided to become vigilantes and had landed on the local news, and here they were at the cop shop, and the heat and chemistry between her and Gabriel was making her question everything.

"Yeah, she keeps saying that." Ruby glanced over to Marty, talking as if she wasn't even there. "She's just afraid of making another mistake, like with MM, except, as I told her, if she keeps living in fear, she'll be alone." Then Ruby turned to face her, and Elizabeth couldn't get her tongue to move, because she couldn't believe how everyone was trying to push her and Gabriel together. "Seriously, Lizzie, you need to give yourself a break and take a look at that handsome guy who's got your back, and don't forget, we know you. There's no way you can hide the fact that you're interested in Gabriel. The chemistry rocks, and you know what? You two seriously are pretty together."

This was worse!

She could feel Gabriel behind her, and she wondered if her sister could tell by the way her eyes widened that Elizabeth wanted to kick her ass. Maybe she did, as a mischievous smile touched her lips, and before she could say anything else, there was a knock on the door and the sheriff opened it. Elizabeth could hear her mother carrying on outside, but she couldn't hear exactly what was being said.

"Okay, Ruby, Marty, Elizabeth, your parents are here," Blake said, and Elizabeth felt her jaw slacken when she heard the commotion. Her mother appeared first in the doorway, wearing a bright pink skirt and a white short-sleeved blouse. Her hair was a brown poof that looked as if she'd just come from the salon, and her face was thick with makeup.

"Oh, you two, whatever did happen?" Chloe said. "It's all over the news, and every neighbor in the hood is talking.

Your dad and I just had a word here with… Oh, Gabriel, so nice to see you." Her mom actually pivoted, strode to Gabriel, and offered her cheek for him to kiss.

Elizabeth wanted to die in embarrassment, and her hands flew up to her face of their own accord. Gabriel actually kissed her mother's cheek as she patted his shoulder.

"As I was saying, I was talking to your daddy out there. What a good man, coming down here to help out my Ruby and Marty, and all for you, Elizabeth. Why, that there just shows you what a good family, good people they are. And my grand-baby is right now out at your family's ranch and being looked after." Her mom was still talking as Elizabeth took in Andy in the doorway, an amused smile on his face, her dad behind him.

The sheriff was leaning against an old file cabinet, his arms crossed, and he lifted his hand as if he realized no one was going to let him get a word in edgewise. "Okay, I'm going to have to cut in here, Mrs. Abercrombie…" he said, as her mom was holding center stage and was taking a breath to carry on with something Elizabeth knew would further embarrass her.

"Oh, Chloe, please, sheriff," her mother said. "We don't stand on formalities here. Isn't that right, Frank? Come on, get on in here. You two stirred up quite a hornet's nest, but the sheriff here was just telling us that he's talked to the owner of that place, and he's agreed to drop all charges…"

"As I was saying, how about you let me finish telling them, Chloe?" Blake said. Elizabeth noted the calm tone he took with her mother, who then lifted her hands as if she was allowing him to speak. Elizabeth found herself stepping over to the desk beside Gabriel. His glance to her lingered a little long and unsettled her.

"Of course, by all means, Sheriff," Chloe added, and Elizabeth didn't miss her sister's laugh.

"There are damages that have to be paid, a few hundred, and you promise never to go into the Waddling Pig again, and you get to walk away with no charges," Blake said, taking them all in.

Elizabeth took in the exchange between her brother and sister. "Deal," Ruby said, and her brother just shrugged as if it were no problem.

"I'll pay for it," Elizabeth said, feeling everyone's eyes on her. "It's only right. They were only there because of me."

"You're not paying for it," Gabriel said just as her brother and sister leveled a heavy gaze her way.

"He's right, Lizzie," Ruby said. "You can barely pay for groceries. I lost my temper. I'm the one who threw the first punch."

She could see the sheriff take in her sister, and she wondered for a minute if he was considering the possibility of the trouble she could be. Then he lifted his hand again as if he realized how her family could go on and on and he'd never get them out of there.

"Then there's MM," he said before anyone could add anything else, and Elizabeth couldn't help the way she moved closer to Gabriel, his hand reaching over and resting on hers. "We're letting him go, releasing him, since, as Ruby said, she threw the first punch. He did hit her, but you see, the thing is that charges could be reciprocal, Ruby and MM."

She took in the moment her mom understood, and her sister too.

"So no one's pressing any charges," Blake said, "and you all go home. You all agree to stay away from each other."

Gabriel took her hand and held it, and she couldn't tear her eyes away from him. "Okay, so everyone walks away, but isn't the whole point of this that MM won't leave Elizabeth alone? So how is it that you're going to get him to agree to all of this?"

"Well, for one, before he's released, we plan on having a talk with him," Andy said, stepping inside the office and resting his arm up on the file cabinet. She took in the exchange with the sheriff, realizing something more had been said. "We'll convince him and help him understand how it's in his best interest to move on."

She didn't know why, but the way Andy spoke, she believed he could make it happen. The edge of ruthlessness she thought she'd seen when she'd first met him was back, and it was something about him that made her damn nervous. Gabriel glanced down at her, and she took in the intensity in the mixed blue green of his eyes, which had her breath catching.

"Yeah, and I'll be there too," he said to everyone, but he looked only at Elizabeth.

When she opened her mouth to tell him *What? No, it's not your problem*, all that came out was, "Thank you."

Chapter Twenty

Gabriel turned off the truck and slid around in the bench seat, taking in Elizabeth as she sat in the passenger side. The night had settled in. It was dark, and he didn't say anything for a minute. He took her in, feeling as if he could just reach out and pull her closer. She wished he would, but she said nothing.

"We really should get Shaunty," she said. "It's not right that your mom and dad keep her tonight."

She wasn't sure what expression was on his face, but he just shook his head, stepped out of the truck, and walked around the front. What the hell was that?

She pulled open the door just as he came around, and he slid his hands around her as she stepped out, pulling her closer, running his hands over her back and lower, over her ass. He lowered his head and pressed a kiss to her lips, and she couldn't keep from leaning into it, taking it deeper, or maybe it was him. She sighed into it as her hands slid over his shoulders, and she was pulled closer, feeling every hard, chiseled part of him.

Then he broke the kiss and lifted his head just a bit,

and she didn't miss the heat in his eyes. "No more talking about Shaunty," he said. "I told you she's already in bed, asleep, and we'll get her tomorrow. Besides…" He just took her in, and she could feel the way her heart hammered harder and wondered if he could feel it, her reaction to him, which she couldn't hide anymore. She wasn't sure when it had happened, at what point she hadn't wanted to fight this attraction—no, this need to allow herself to be happy.

He reached for her hand and led her up the steps to the house, then let go only long enough to shove the key in the door and pull her in. He pressed the door closed and turned the deadbolt before turning everything in his gaze on her.

She swallowed and could feel her insides shaking, but it wasn't from cold, and she wondered, as his gaze lingered on her, whether he had any idea how she was feeling. His hand lifted to her chin, sliding over the edge of her jawline and over her lips, and she didn't look away, though his gaze should have had her backing away, because it said every-thing about what was going to happen in a matter of seconds.

"We can't do this," she said. "It's not right. There are all kinds of boundaries here that we're crossing, and we can't. I don't want to ruin—"

He lifted his finger and pressed it over her lips, so she stopped talking. For a minute, he seemed angry. Then he stepped away from her, into the living room, jamming his hands in his hair and yanking hard before he dropped them to his sides. She stared at his fists, seeing a side of him she hadn't before.

"You know what?" he said. "Would you just stop already with this boundaries crap? Haven't I shown you how I feel? Haven't I shown you that I'm not some scumbag? Please explain to me why it is that you keep pushing me away and putting up these walls, saying this can't happen, when just looking at you and seeing your reaction to me, I can see that all of this is just bullshit, as if you're trying to convince yourself there can't be anything between us."

He started toward her, and she stepped back until she bumped the wall. He was right in front of her, pressing into her, and she could feel all his hardness, so much that her legs felt limp, and for a second she thought they'd give way if he hadn't been standing so close and pressed to her, holding her up. She lifted her hands over his chest, feeling the pulse of his heart, feeling the sharp cut of his pecs, wondering what his abs looked like and feeling all that flat hardness pressed against her.

Her fingers wrapped in the cotton of his shirt, and she couldn't fight the need to just touch him. He lowered his head again to kiss her, and she turned her head and pressed his chest until he stepped back. She could move around him even though her body wept, and she felt his hand brush over her arm as he groaned in frustration, but that sound was nothing compared to how frustrated she was with herself. She couldn't look at him, and she had her hands on her face, her eyes shut, as she tried to remember why it was so important for her to be who she was and not ever take a chance again on something that couldn't work.

She dropped her hands and turned around, seeing the way he lingered a foot away, maybe more, and his expression showed how close he was to losing his calm. Maybe she could push harder, and anything he didn't want to show would appear, that hidden monster that he'd carefully tucked away, before she was in too deep—before she fell hard for him and he let it slip, crushing her heart. It was just a matter of time, she supposed. She was done with the lies, the deception, and the crazy, yet there he was, not doing what she expected him to.

"Maybe you say it's not so, that you're decent and kind and this is the real you, but how hard do I have to push before I see something you don't want me to see?" she said.

It was in his expression, the shock, and he pulled back as if he was done with her. It was what she'd tried so hard for, what she'd really wanted, but at the same time, right now, she was angry at herself for bringing about something she seemed to be destined for.

"What is it exactly that you think I'm hiding, huh?" he said. He stalked toward her, and she took in his strong arms, the muscles of his forearms, the strength that oozed out of him. She stood there, looking up at him, as he stopped right in front of her, so close that she could feel his warm breath. She wanted everything about him so bad.

"I can see now how angry you are with me," she said. "You can't hide it. Are you going to tell me to go? Or maybe after you have me in bed a few times and I open my heart to you, you'll decide it's not what you want, but having me here is easy. I'll give myself to you again and again, but you'll pull away after all the kind words, the chase, and then you …" She stopped talking, because it wasn't just anger she saw on his face. It was something she didn't understand looking back at her.

"Elizabeth, I'm not your ex. I'm not the kind of guy who gets a kick out of toying with a woman and her heart. If this is what you think is going to happen with us, if you expect this from every man, the deceit, the unfaithfulness, and all that crap you put up with from someone who didn't deserve you, then you're right: You will always believe that love is for fools, because you've already made your mind up that there can't be anything else between us and that I've got some evil twisted side that I'm hiding and am going to pull the rug out from under you. The problem is, Elizabeth, that isn't me, and I just realized there's nothing I can do to convince you. There's nothing I can do to show you that we can have something really good." He lifted his hands and then dropped them to his sides, brushing his jeans, and he suddenly looked so tired as he turned away from her.

Then he did something she didn't expect. He lifted his hands in the air and backed up. "You know what? I'm going to bed," he said, and it left a little part of her broken as sadness took over his amazing eyes, and she was responsible for putting it there. Then he turned away and started down the hall.

"Gabriel," she said, her hand on her chest, wanting to go to him, wanting to say she was sorry, wanting to take what he was offering, but as he turned his head, glancing to her, all she could say was, "Never mind."

Chapter Twenty-One

He rested his arm on the window frame, taking in his darkened backyard and the silence in the house, realizing with sadness that Elizabeth just might be too far gone to give any chance to love. Could he blame her? Not really, he thought, remembering the moment he, Blake, and his dad had stepped into the concrete interrogation room in the back of the sheriff's office after leaving Elizabeth, her siblings, and her parents in Blake's office to dissect the drama of the fight at the Waddling Pig.

There, they'd found an arrogant Mac Murrin sprawled in a chair without an ounce of remorse. The door had shut, and he'd said not a word as an easy smile touched the sides of his lips. The guy had confidence if not brains. Any sane person would have been shitting his pants, considering the gravity of the situation.

"So what is this…?" MM said and narrowed his gaze on Gabriel, and he knew the moment he realized who he was. "Oh, you. Shit, dog, you think you can go after what's mine?" He actually sneered at Gabriel, and his dad had stiffened, and Blake too, as if they believed he would try something.

"Well, that's the thing," Gabriel said. "Elizabeth isn't yours."

MM laughed, and Andy moved around the room and stood across from him, not saying a word, though his expression said that he wasn't one to mess with. "See, that's where you're confused," MM said. "Lizzie is mine. She has my kid, which makes her my property."

He couldn't believe he'd actually said that. "Seriously? You were with another chick in the bar, yet you think Elizabeth and you are together? You're delusional, and you don't own her. You have no rights, and she's clearly asked you to stay away from her."

"She's a woman. She doesn't know what she wants," he said dryly, and Gabriel realized the guy actually believed it.

"So let me get this straight. You want Elizabeth back, but you're messing around with someone else…"

"They're just women," MM said.

"Well, this is going nowhere," Blake said. "Let me be clear, Mr. Murrin: This is the last time I want to see you in my station, and I've already warned you to stay away from Elizabeth. Now I'm going to be really clear. Elizabeth has made her feelings clear, and you're done, so you pursuing her, contacting her…"

"She has my kid. I have every right!" MM said, cutting the sheriff off, and even Gabriel saw the man wasn't about to go quietly into the night.

"Seeing your kid doesn't mean you get to harass Elizabeth," Blake said. "That's an entirely different matter. Get your lawyer to work out visitation, but you won't contact Elizabeth again. You work at the shipping yard. Wasn't it just this year that a big bust went down where the Feds seized guns, drugs, and other illegal contraband? They arrested some small-time employees, but no one was talking about who was really behind it."

Something then passed between the sheriff and his dad, and a hint of a smile touched one side of Andy's mouth. Gabriel knew it was more a warning to Mac Murrin that he was messing with the wrong man.

"Guess Jason Mears hasn't had the right incentive to bring the guilty party out. Could be worth a talk to him," Andy said. Was that MM's boss at the yard? Gabriel just stared, realizing what they were saying. MM was suddenly quiet as if he'd figured out how bad this could be.

"Look, I had nothing to do with that. Mr. Mears isn't going to start pointing fingers…"

"Oh, he will with the right incentive," Andy said, and Blake just inclined his head as if in total agreement. Andy pulled out his phone and started dialing—who, Gabriel didn't have a clue, since he'd been under the impression they were going in to see Mac for a talk, yet he suddenly felt as if they'd forgotten to give him the script.

"Oh, I see where this is going. Pretend to call, try and bust my balls," MM said. "No, sorry, I think I won't bite, and I'll call your bluff."

His dad didn't even blink. "Jason, Andy Friessen. Yeah, great. Meant to ask how your daughter's graduation went." His father never took his eyes off MM, and even Gabriel could see the bullshit arrogant side of him was starting to slip. "Right, right. We should meet for drinks soon. Listen, I've got a little problem here. I'm sitting in front of one of your yard workers, Mac Murrin…"

"You win," Mac snarled. "Hang up the phone."

Blake gestured to Andy, who nodded and said, "Yeah, hoping there isn't a problem. Listen, let me give you a call back. We may have just resolved the situation. Sure, you bet, Friday." Then he hung up and stared down at MM, who lifted his hands.

"You want her, she's yours," he said, taking in Gabriel, the sheriff, and Andy.

"Great, so you stay away from Elizabeth," Andy said, resting his hands on the tabletop, "and then we'll have no more issues. It would be so easy to have another conversation with Jason where I'll make sure something happens that you do need to be afraid of. Do we understand each other?"

It had been that simple, that easy, finding the one thing that would hit MM where it hurt: his fear of being locked up for something he may or may not have done. Gabriel had seen firsthand how far his dad would go for one of them, and he considered only a second what he'd done for Elizabeth, who was now in bed on one of those ridiculous air mattresses, likely with her boundaries erected, cast in stone.

She'd made it clear there could be no future between them, and he didn't know what else to do to convince her or show her that insanity and craziness wouldn't darken their doorstep or rip her life apart again.

There was a tap on his bedroom door, and he frowned in the dark as it opened and he spotted the silhouette of Elizabeth.

"I'm sorry," she said, and her voice sounded so raw and sad.

He didn't move from where he leaned against the window, and he didn't make an effort to turn on the light as she stepped into the room and crossed it to him. He could see she was barefoot, still wearing her loose blue jeans and sleeveless blouse. Her hair hung in soft messy waves.

"I'm scared," she said. "I don't want to ever step into

something thinking it's good and then it turns out I'm in a relationship that isn't going to work for me and the person I fell in love with turns out to be hiding a dark side."

"Elizabeth…" he started, and she hurried toward him, pressing her hand to his mouth. Maybe she could hear the irritation in his voice.

"No, Gabriel, let me finish, because if I don't say this, I don't think I'll have the nerve to say it."

He realized her hand was shaking as she allowed it to fall away and lowered it to her side.

"I've always dreamed of meeting that perfect guy, that perfect partner who would have my back. I just never expected to meet you. And I keep telling myself that you're hiding something, some part of you that you don't want me to see, and you're only showing me the good part of you, and then I'll fall for you hard and I'll realize it's all a lie."

He drew a breath, knowing he sounded impatient.

She lifted her startled gaze to him, her eyes wide. "But that's the thing. It's too late. I already fell for you, and I just couldn't admit it to myself. I've been comparing you to MM, and for that I'm sorry, because you've done nothing to show me you're like him. Maybe because I've been hounded by him for so long, his crazy behavior, and he won't leave me alone, I'm seeing the worst, his worst, in you. But it isn't you. I guess I'm saying I'm scared, but at the same time, Gabriel, I'm tired of being scared, and I really, really want something good and to take a chance again. I want to be happy. I deserve to be happy," she said, then just stopped talking, and he wasn't sure what to say, because he wasn't sure she was saying what he thought she was.

"Are you done talking?" he asked, and she didn't say a word, only nodded, so he said, "Fine."

He stepped closer to her, putting his hands over her shoulders and leaning in. He dragged his hands up and around her cheeks, her ears, holding her so she had to look up at him. Her lips were so close, and it was only the hint of light from the stars outside that allowed him to see the glitter in her eyes. There was such passion there, and he realized she'd likely hid it away. Right now he wanted her to feel safe with him, to let down that guard so he could be with the Elizabeth who was hidden behind those thick walls she'd erected out of necessity.

He pressed a kiss to her lips, holding her as she draped her arms over his shoulders. She moved in closer as she deepened the kiss, and he tasted her, his hands running freely down her shoulders and around her back, over her ass, feeling the perfection. She groaned in the kiss as she ran her hands over his chest, and it was her touch, her energy, that he couldn't seem to get enough of. He thought he'd go blind with need if he didn't get her into bed, and at the same time he didn't want to push too hard. Baby steps, but he didn't want to wait.

Elizabeth stepped back and then slid her hand in his and started over to his bed.

"Are you sure?" he said, wanting to kick himself for giving her an out.

She didn't say anything as she flicked the button on her blouse and then another until it fell open, and he took in her lacy cupped bra and her breasts spilling out. He was dying to touch and feel and taste them. Then her hands were on the edge of his T-shirt, lifting it up. "Do you want to talk, or do you want to get into bed?" he said.

He wanted to strip her down. His hands slipped under her open shirt and pushed it off her shoulders, and then he unhooked her bra and pulled it away. He pulled his shirt over his head, and Elizabeth slipped out of her jeans and crawled onto the bed naked, lying on her back and pulling her leg up as she waited for him.

He didn't know how he did it, taking his time as he took in her perfection, slowly dropping his zipper and stepping out of his jeans and underwear, thick and ready for her. He walked over to the bedside table and pulled open the drawer, then reached for a condom wrapper and tossed it on the bed beside her.

"One of us needs to be thinking," he said as he climbed over her, holding himself up, and he pressed his body to her. She kissed him deeply, her sweet mouth, her soft gasps as he took his time touching every part of her, tasting her, kissing her, exploring her before covering himself and sliding inside her. It was that first time, that first time being with her, inside her, moving with her, that he just knew she was the one.

And then it happened, the first time he saw her.

The entire family was congregated at the ranch. It had taken Elizabeth some time to really understand how close Gabriel was to his family and how they had welcomed her and Shaunty into the fold. There was no craziness, no more having to always watch over her shoulder, fearing the other shoe would drop and MM would suddenly appear and stir up shit, demanding she come back. In fact, she hadn't seen or heard from him again, and Gabriel had said she wouldn't have to worry, that he wouldn't bother her. She'd asked what he'd done, how he could know for sure, and she remembered his exact words:

"We made sure he understood clearly it was in his best interest to walk away."

That was all he'd said to her, and she hadn't asked more, still expecting that MM would show up, because no one had ever been able to get through to her before.

"Thought you would like some white wine," said Laura, Gabriel's mother, who was holding two glasses. She had long blond hair and was slim and curvy in a loose pair of jeans and a sleeveless pink blouse, absolutely gorgeous, with the most amazing green eyes Elizabeth had ever seen.

"Thank you," Elizabeth said, taking the glass. Shaunty was with Gabriel over by the corral, where Andy was on horseback along with Jeremy, separating some of the cattle into another pen. Sarah was manning some chute, and Chelsea was standing off by herself a little further down the rails, quiet and brooding, her long dark hair tucked under a cowboy hat. She wore ultra-short shorts and a tank top, with her feet shoved in boots. She was the one Friessen Elizabeth hadn't been able to figure out and get to know.

"Your little girl reminds me so much of Chelsea, smart, curious," Laura said, "but she has Sarah's sweetness. She was the easy one. Zachary over there argued about everything the moment he could talk."

Elizabeth took in the youngest Friessen, who was sitting atop the rails, saying something to his dad, who had a big smile on his face. Just watching them all together, seeing how close they were, this big family, she suddenly realized she was a part of them now.

"Then there's Jeremy…" Laura said. "He is so much like his father, there are days I swear his personality was poured from the same cast."

Elizabeth took in this mother who loved her children so deeply. "Shaunty loves coming here," she said. "You and Andy spoil her, and she always asks Gabriel when we're coming back." She took in the wide smile on Laura's face and the love there in her expression, how it softened as she looked out to her husband. What an incredible love affair they'd had. Every time she was around them, she didn't miss the way he always touched her, a kiss here or there, his hand on her ass or around her, pulling her closer. The way they looked at each other and laughed, she could see now why Gabriel was who he was. She lifted her glass and took a swallow of wine.

"We'd take her anytime," Laura said. "She's always welcome here. We love having her. You know you make Gabriel very happy, but sometimes I look at you and wonder if you believe it's okay to love him back."

Elizabeth nearly choked and coughed as the wine went down the wrong way, then took a second to understand what his mother was saying. Laura reached over and rubbed her back as she said, "Really?" Her voice was raspy, and she took another swallow of wine to clear her throat.

Laura didn't say anything, and Elizabeth wasn't sure what to make of the expression on her face.

"I do love him," she said, "but you're right. I've been waiting for the other shoe to drop. You know when you live with something so bad for so long, you just have that expectation that something bad is going to happen—that MM is going to show up at Gabriel's and go all psycho and hurt him. I can't seem to shake it, so it's still there even though I know Gabriel and your husband and the sheriff had a talk with him, even though Gabriel said he was gone and wouldn't be back. I just know that he doesn't give up, that…"

Laura reached over and rested her hand on her wrist, an odd smile pulling at her lips. "Oh, that," she said, and for a minute Elizabeth wasn't sure whether she was going to laugh or what. "You know, when my husband came home and told me what happened at the station and the talk they had with your ex, I knew what he'd done without him having to explain in detail. Let's just say I know my husband well, and he'll do anything to protect his family, us. Gabriel has learned from his father how to be a man, a good man. I know your ex won't bother you. You can be sure of that. It took me a lot of years to understand the man Andy is, a lot of years for me to shake my own fear that I see on your face. Let it go, Elizabeth."

Elizabeth took in Laura, who was so young, so kind and loving, and then Gabriel, who was walking their way with Shaunty, who was giggling as she sat on his shoulders. Then she felt her hand on her back.

"Go on, be with my son," Laura said. "Go be happy, and take it from me: My son is the real deal."

She watched as Laura strode down the stairs and said something to Gabriel, who lifted Shaunty off his shoulders and set her down on the ground. Laura took her hand and walked over to the corral, leaving Gabriel and Elizabeth alone. Then he was up the steps, standing right in front of her, and she took in his perfection.

"So can I interest you in a ride?" he said before he leaned in and kissed her.

She laughed and lifted her hand up to his cheek. "Sure. Just so you know, I've never been on a horse before."

He pulled her closer, his arms around her, settling on her waist. "We'll just add it to the list, one more thing I'm going to have fun teaching you."

Turn the page for a sneak peek of
WELCOME TO MY ARMS the next book in *THE FRIESSENS*
Available in print, eBook & audio

Everyone in Columbia Falls, Montana believes that Chelsea Friessen is a spoiled princess who is more trouble than she's worth. They'd be wrong though, considering that tale was spun by a scorned high school crush and two years later is still the first impression everyone has of her.

But when she meets a man whose personality is as arrogant as he is drop dead gorgeous that if Chelsea was in her right mind should have her running away from him. The only problem is that this badass stranger walked into her life knowing he saved her from humiliation, a stranger and a kiss she couldn't resist where he pretended to be her fiancé. The only problem with pretending is it suddenly becomes far too real.

Chapter 1

A strong man can handle a strong woman. A weak man will tell everyone that she has an attitude, is a troublemaker or a spoiled princess, and is downright bad news, just waiting for the opportunity to bring a man to his knees. Chelsea Friessen had grown up with the first type, and she'd dated the second.

But then, her father had ruined her by setting the bar for men ridiculously high, which was why she was in her current predicament. Where was she? At Whitefish Lake, half an hour from home, perched at the edge of a dock, her feet dangling in the glacial lake water, still cold even in August, wearing a bikini that had her looking especially hot. She held a journal and pen and was scribbling down reminders that she wasn't an epic failure, all the while doing her best to ignore Boone Hudson—blond, tall, totally fucking ripped, and the source of all her misery.

She should have known. What good could ever come of dating someone named Boone? He spent more time in front of a mirror than a woman ever could.

"You can't sit there all day, you know," said Paige Jenkins-Morris, Chelsea's best friend since middle school, whose mother had insisted on the importance of a hyphenated last name. Paige was roughly a size twelve, stuffed in a yellow and pink bikini, and she didn't give a crap how she looked to anyone. Her jet-black hair was tied into a stubby ponytail, and she was wearing thick sunglasses and had, until seconds ago, appeared to be sleeping.

Paige lifted her head and pulled down the shades, her dark eyes packing a punch as she stared at Chelsea with a gaze that told her to stop giving a fuck what everyone thought. "And while you're at it, put down that journal and pen. You look ridiculous. You're supposed to be sunning yourself and having fun, remember? Grab that other air mattress and get on down here instead of sitting up there, burying your head in that journal, writing God knows what, and ruining my day off."

She wondered whether Paige had any idea how ironic it was that she was calling out Chelsea for looking ridiculous, considering she was the one with streaks of sunscreen all over her dark skin. "For your information," she said, "I'm making notes and finding a way to redirect my focus."

She heard laughing and knew it was coming from Boone and the crowd of jocks at the other end of the dock, like ten feet from where she sat. It was a group that hadn't changed in years, one she'd once hung with when she'd been Boone's girlfriend. She wondered too whether the sweat beading under her arms from their nonstop ridicule would start dripping down her sides. Hate was hate, and he and his friends never let an opportunity pass to cut her down.

"You're only encouraging them, Chels, by sitting up there, getting all worked up, pretending not to care—and you're not fooling me. You're still letting him affect you."

"How is that, when I'm sitting here minding my own

business? I'm not even looking their way. And, for that matter, why didn't you tell me he was going to be here?" She could feel the bite of her words as she lowered her voice, wanting to yell at her friend. Paige must have known, though, as she didn't pull away her gaze, which never missed anything.

"Caused any other guys trouble lately, Chelsea?" called out one of the guys with Boone, and then they were laughing again.

Chelsea could feel her cheeks burning. Paige still was staring at her, but this time she shifted her pointed gaze to Boone and his friends. Chelsea could feel their gazes burning a hole in her back, knowing they were still about fifty feet away from her.

"What are you writing, Chelsea? New ways you can torment some poor guy and turn his life to shit, cause him problems? Or maybe you're thinking up new ways to fuck a guy over." It wasn't Boone who'd said it, but it could have been, considering those were his words.

"You think she's putting on a little weight?" That time it was Boone, and she despised him for being such a hateful prick.

"Ignore them, please," Paige said, "and stop sitting up there being a target. Please, Chelsea."

She knew Paige was right and closed up her book, pressing it against her flat stomach, feeling the sting of their words, remembering the ice cream she'd had earlier. Now she was angry for letting them slap that doubt into her head. *Like, seriously?*

"You said she was cold in bed, couldn't kiss, so when exactly did she turn psycho on you?" one of the guys was saying.

She actually turned her head this time, seeing Boone's expression and the minute he'd realized he'd found a way to get to her. One of his friends cannonballed into the frigid water. They weren't looking right her way anymore, but she knew they weren't going to let up.

"Paige, he just won't stop," she said. "Why does he keep doing this?" She turned back to her friend, trying to understand what she had done to deserve Boone's wrath. No matter how she tried, all his cruel personal digs were beginning to haunt her, and her confidence was taking a nosedive.

"Because he's got a little dick, isn't that what you said?" Paige yelled out, and she wanted to kick her friend for not taking her own advice.

She heard the laughter and again was mortified, because this wasn't helping in the least. "Didn't you say to ignore them?" she snapped. "Again, why didn't you tell me he'd be here?"

"I don't keep tabs on him and when he's out here, but you can't keep avoiding him and his friends. This is our fun too, you know, and you're not sitting at home and hiding out anymore. It's a small town, and you know they're out here most of the summer. It's been two years since he broke it off with you. Stop letting him see he's getting to you. You keep sitting up there doodling like you are when you should be down here chilling like me. Now, get on down here, and let's enjoy this last day of sun and fun before we have to step back into reality and the daily grind of being overworked and underappreciated."

She flicked her pen and closed up her journal, then rested it on the edge of the dock and stood. She could feel eyes on her backside, and for the first time she was wondering whether her bikini bottom was a little snug.

"So what were you writing in that journal, Chelsea?" one of the guys called out. It was Kurt, and she refused to look his way as she reached for the second air mattress tied to the dock. She tossed it beside Paige in the dark lake water, which she wasn't looking forward to getting into. It was the kind of cold that sucked your breath away until you got used to it, even though it was an unusually hot August. She crouched down on the dock and then dangled her legs over the edge, ready to slip into the water, when she felt and heard the footsteps behind her and turned to see Boone coming toward her. He grabbed her black hardcover journal.

"Hey, what do you think you're doing?" She lifted her legs out of the water. There were people in the distance, on the rocky shore, and a few lingering by one of the four boats tied to the dock further down. She felt she was being watched by everyone.

"Boone, you asshole, give that back to her right now!" Paige was outraged behind her, and Chelsea heard the splash of her diving off that plastic air mattress and swimming in.

Boone stepped back as she reached for her journal, holding it up higher, out of her reach, his expression hard and unforgiving.

"Boone, that isn't yours. Give it back right now!"

He stepped back again, lifting his hand and flipping open her book. "'I am strong, I am comfortable in my own skin, I am an amazing person, I deserve to be loved, I am decent...'" He started laughing, and she could feel people staring at her. She wished in that moment the ground would open up and she could slip away.

"Boone, you asshole, those are my private thoughts! You have no right to read that." She jumped up and tried to grab the journal, but he just lifted his other hand out, his arms long and strong, holding her back so she couldn't reach the book he was still reading. His touch did nothing for her anymore other than add to the sick feeling of being publicly humiliated.

"Oh, let's see, where did I leave off? Yeah, this is real deep, Chels. Just shows how shallow you are. 'A real man never stops showing a girl he cares about her, even if he already has her…' Like, what the fuck is that?" He turned the page. How he managed with one hand, she couldn't figure, as she jumped and pushed against him. His other hand brushed over her breast twice.

"Boone, you complete and utter jerk!" Paige shouted from the water as she neared the dock. "You give that back to Chelsea now! This is a new low, even for you."

Boone flicked his gaze to Chelsea, and she saw how unfeeling it was. He hated her, she knew that, but seeing the way he looked at her now, she realized nothing inside him cared even just a little. "You really think any man is going to give you the time of day once they figure out who you really are?" he said.

"Boone, please don't read any more…" Her voice was shaking. She was shaking.

He flicked his gaze back to her book. "'If another woman steals your man, there's no better revenge than letting her keep him. Real men can't be stolen.'" He lifted the book and gave her a disapproving glare. His light hazel eyes, which had once softened her knees, did nothing for her, and then he *tsked*. "What it should say is a guy deserves a fucking bronze star for having survived a twisted relationship with a crazy broad who's a spoiled princess and believes mankind revolves around her."

"Give that back to her right now!" someone said. It was a man's deep voice, and she didn't look over as she took in Boone, who frowned and turned to the side. She didn't know how she did it, but as she pushed against his hand, which was holding her back, it gave just enough for her to rip the book away.

"Hey, this is private, do you mind?" Boone snapped, but Chelsea didn't care. At least she had her book.

"I do mind, actually, because listening to you carry on is getting on my nerves," the man drawled. She took in his dark hair. He wasn't even looking her way.

"What the hell do you care? She deserves a little humiliation for all the problems she caused me," Boone said.

Chelsea clutched the book and looked right and then left. If she slipped away now, would anyone notice? Paige was still struggling to get on the dock rather ungracefully, sliding up on her stomach. She was soaked and appeared madder than a mother bear. Chelsea reached down and gave her a hand.

"Don't be an asshole," the man said. "You don't go around reading anyone's private stuff. That's just hitting below the belt. No one deserves that, dude."

He still wasn't looking her way, this tall, dark, and utterly dangerous guy with a ripped chest and flat abs. He had several inches on Boone and was wearing a pair of loose shorts that hung low on his waist, and he was shirtless. Where the hell had he come from?

He was still giving everything to Boone in that moment, every bit of his hard glance. She wished she could see his eyes, which were hidden behind a pair of Maui Jims. His face was made of hard lines, and he had the kind of expression she knew well.

"Hey, if you knew her, you wouldn't be saying that," Boone said. "Any guy with a lick of sense wouldn't hook up with this prima donna. I'm just doing every red-blooded male out there a favor and saving them from misery. I had the misfortune of dating her, and she made my life a living hell," he snapped.

She could feel how tight her face was, her mouth, as she fought the urge to swallow. The guy glanced her way and then took another step closer. Why couldn't the dock give way right now? Seriously, right now would be about the best time for a natural disaster of sorts to strike and end her humiliation.

"Know her? I know her well," the man said. "Don't have a clue what you're getting at, but sounds to me as if you're the one with the problem."

Had he seriously just said he knew her? He had all her attention now, but not even a smile touched his lips. What the fuck was this? She could feel her mouth gaping. He stepped in closer again until he was right beside her, and what did Boone do? She didn't need to look his way to see how rattled he was. Either way, she couldn't tear her eyes from the dangerous stranger. Then she heard Boone laugh.

"Oh, you're shitting me. Man, dude, I don't know if I should feel sorry for you or help you dig your grave." Boone lifted his hands again, and she could see how flustered he was. Then he actually jabbed a finger in her direction, and she couldn't remember ever being so mortified. "Hey, your funeral, but if you really knew her, I think you'd be running the other way."

The stranger slid his hand around her, over her hip, and pulled her closer, right against him and his rock-hard wall of muscles. "Well, that's the thing, dickhead. I do know her well, very well."

She didn't know whether the shock on her face was in fact mirroring Boone's. Paige, too, whom she caught out of the corner of her eye, wore an expression she didn't think she'd ever seen before.

"And if you ever disrespect my fiancée again," the man said, "I'll see to it that you don't eat solid food for at least six to eight weeks, because your broken jaw will be wired shut. I, for one, will be doing everyone a favor so they don't have to listen to you trash talk anyone. Capisce?"

She couldn't pull her eyes from the stranger who had his arm around her. He was hotter than all hell, and he had basically saved her from ridicule, putting Boone in his place—and he'd called her his fiancée! Like, what the fuck?

He was looking at her now, but she couldn't see his eyes from behind those sunglasses. That damn book was still between them as he lifted his hand over her shoulder and traced it down her arm. "You almost done, babe?" he said.

All she could do was stare, and, seeing Paige standing just behind the guy, she knew her friend was likely more stunned than she was.

"Uh…yeah," she managed to say, and then he leaned in and pressed his lips to hers, pulling her closer into a kiss that went from zero to, like, six hundred. Holy shit, could he kiss!

When he pulled back, she dropped her journal, and for the life of her, she didn't know what the hell to say.

Chapter 2

WELCOME TO MY ARMS

"So, again, tell me how you don't know him?" Paige said.

Chelsea kept both her hands wrapped around the steering wheel of her dad's pickup. The air conditioning was blasting, and she shivered in her bulky white T-shirt and cut-offs, feeling gritty and sweaty on the soft leather seats, wanting a cool shower and some quiet time to digest what had happened.

She didn't have to look Paige's way to know that she was thrown, considering she hadn't stopped with the accusations for the whole ride.

"I don't know him!" Chelsea said. "I swear I've never seen him before."

She was still rattled from all of it: his kiss, his touch. She could say without a doubt that she'd never been kissed like that, ever! Even the way his hand had so intimately traced its way over her bare skin, her arm, her shoulder, her lower back, and her ass, it was as if he'd touched her countless times, like a fiancé would have.

"Then explain to me why a total stranger would just

step in the way he did and basically save your ass. I mean, did you see him? He was totally ripped, fucking ripped—a Greek god who would have and could have easily kicked Boone's ass and not even broken a sweat! And did you see the way Boone slinked off? Even his friends, every one of them. That guy totally and one hundred percent shut them all down, like in two seconds flat."

This time she did glance to Paige, whose expression was showing the same shock Chelsea was very much still feeling. It was taking everything she had to keep herself in this seat and at the speed limit without going on and on like Paige was.

"I know. I was there with you, remember?" Chelsea said. "I did see the way he looked. In fact, I was the one in that kiss. Did you see how Boone and his friends packed up and left? I honestly don't know why that stranger would step in and do what he did."

That was another reason she was the mess she was, being touched like that, kissed like that. She still didn't even know the guy's name.

"And then he just left—left!"

Yeah, she'd seen that. After she pulled her gaze away from Boone and his friends, who'd jumped off the dock and headed to the parking lot, the stranger had stepped back, leaned down, picked up her journal, brushed it off, and handed it to her. He hadn't removed his shades and never even offered her a smile, a name, a hello, nothing! He'd stared down at her through those mirrored shades, his face completely unreadable, before turning and walking back to where the boats were on the other side of the dock, disappearing into a crowd of strangers.

She'd just stood there like a frickin' idiot, unable to say a word, to move, as she clutched her big bulky journal. Basically, she'd been shell shocked.

"Did you see which boat he got into?" Paige said. Her energy was still ramped up, and Chelsea had to fight to keep her eyes on the road as she slowed for the turn to the ranch, where Paige had left her little red compact.

"Actually, he didn't get on a boat. I saw him head toward the condos. You should've gone after him, that fine piece of male—"

"Yeah, no!" She cut off her friend, who was now laughing, knowing exactly where this was going. There was no way she was chasing down some stranger who'd basically saved her and given her the kiss of her life. She was angry at herself because the way he touched her, kissed her, she was wanting it again.

"So you don't know his name?" Paige said.

Was she serious? Chelsea glanced her way and watched as she lifted her hands in the air, and she spotted the humor on her face.

"Sorry, okay, but you know what? I bet his name is, like, Deke or Damian. Yeah, Damian… That is such a hot guy's name." Her friend was fanning her face with her hand.

"Seriously, Paige, I have no idea what his name is or who he is. I've never seen him before and will likely never see him again. There were tons of visitors there from all over, not just us locals. Which…oh, shit."

She lifted her foot from the gas as she slowed on the dirt road, seeing the ranch in the distance. Her mom's minivan was there, as were the horses and cattle, and she could see who she thought were her dad and brother on horseback. The realization hit her fast and hard like a curveball, slamming into her.

"What?" Paige said.

"He said fiancée, remember? I'm his fiancée, getting married. Don't you think that's a problem? I have no idea who that guy was, I don't know his name, and I'll never see him again. Him announcing that he and I are getting married is a very real problem. It'll be all around town, the news of me being engaged, and yet here I am, very much alone. That'll only add fuel to what Boone was saying about how I'm worthless and can't keep a man, how I lose them as soon as they figure out what a problem I am. With this guy all but disappearing, Boone can say, 'See? Told you,' and people will believe him. When people start asking me for his name, who he is, and when I'm getting married, and I can't produce this guy—and, worse, they never see him with me…"

She let it linger, taking in Paige's frown. Maybe she didn't get how dire this was. Chelsea had to fight the urge to lift her hand from the wheel as the butterflies in her stomach started pummeling it like crazy. "There's no guy dating me, and you know what? Everyone is going to say, 'Geeze, maybe Boone is right. Maybe the boy had a point.' Maybe it's all true, every hurtful, cutting, cruel lie he's told about me. People will believe it all—that I'm difficult, deceitful. It'll be there in every look they give me. They'll be thinking it, and every opportunity I might have will be gone. Doors will shut, and everyone will say that Chelsea Friessen is the biggest loser yet."

Chelsea pulled up and parked in front of the sprawling rancher she had grown up in, knowing her mom was somewhere in the house. She turned off the truck, pulled the key from the ignition, and slid off the seatbelt, seeing a deep-thinking Paige in the passenger side, staring out the window.

"All right, I'll give you that," Paige said, "but let me point out that there's a solution to all of this." She unbelted her seatbelt and reached for the yellow beach bag at her feet as she turned and faced Chelsea.

"And that is?" She was dying to know what divine

intervention Paige had received to dig her out of this mess and save her from any further humiliation. She waited, and Paige tapped her chin with her finger.

"You tell everyone you met him in Atlanta and that he travels a lot for business, that he's this hotshot sales rep for a biochemical company, and his name is… Ah, wait." Paige slapped her hands together, and Chelsea waited for whatever crazy-ass name her friend was going to utter. "Adonte! His name is Adonte. Yes, that's it. Ooh, ooh! This is even better. Adonte Corleone, like from *The Godfather*! That's so perfect. It'll have everyone shutting right up."

She felt her jaw slacken and pulled at the handle of the door, seeing her dad and Gabriel still on horseback, heading toward the barn.

"No," she said. "First off, no one our age has even seen *The Godfather*, and there's no way we're telling anyone this, making the guy into some mafia king…so not going to happen. We say nothing, do you hear me? We'll ignore everyone about all of this. It'll die down, and eventually everyone will forget what happened. No names, no story, nothing." Chelsea punctuated the last point, seeing all the excitement in her friend's face fade as she opened her door.

Paige was staring her down, ready to argue, likely, and then she made a face. "And when everyone starts asking about your drop-dead gorgeous fiancé, you think you're going to…what, change the subject, ignore everyone? Seriously? You know that won't fly. Come on, Chelsea. You need to get with the program. You need to come up with a story, one that will stick, one we both know so there are no holes, and one that sounds believable."

Chelsea climbed out of the truck and opened up the back door. She reached for her bag, feeling the weight of the journal, the journal that had been the source of her humiliation. She should really leave it at home from now on so that her private thoughts could never fall into the wrong hands again. "Fine, but you're not calling him Adonte Corleone. That's just not believable."

She didn't need to look over to see that her friend, who was now out of the truck, was grinning from ear to ear as if she'd won some major debate. Chelsea closed the back door and walked around, seeing the excitement brewing in Paige, who had slipped on a long faded yellow and peach swimsuit cover. Her cheap drugstore sunglasses were perched on top of her dark hair, which was wild and out of control, millions of tight curls springing free from her ponytail and sticking out in every direction.

"How about Damian? I just love that name." There was mischief in her dark eyes, and Chelsea could see Paige was likely enjoying this far too much.

She just shook her head. "Nothing dramatic. I want simple, easy, something forgettable. One day, a ways down the road, when everyone has forgotten because something bigger and better has happened, I can just say it didn't work out. His name will be Rob, and he's from Seattle, an engineer. His last name will be Harris. Simple, but not too simple. We met at a party in the summer. We see each other on weekends or as often as we can. It's mostly me going to Seattle, because he doesn't have time to come here. That's it, no more…" She held up her hand when Paige went to add something. "No. That's it: simple, easy, forgettable."

She walked beside Paige to her red older compact and waited as she reached for her keys and pulled open the back door, the hinges groaning. She tossed in her bag.

"You're no fun," Paige said. "We could have really played this up."

Yeah, no. That was exactly what she wasn't going to

do. She'd had enough drama of every kind to last her a lifetime.

"So, Chelsea, didn't know you were getting married."

She hadn't known Jeremy was there. Her twin was on the porch, leaning on the railing, his dark hair a mess. His face had that dangerous look of two days without shaving, and he was looking more and more the spitting image of her father every day. He was in a faded T-shirt and worn jeans, holding a can of soda.

"What the hell, Jeremy? Were you spying on me?" She squeezed the strap of her beach bag, watching as he lifted his other hand, which was holding his cell phone. He didn't need to say any more.

"Imagine my surprise when I get a text from Kurt that he just heard my sister was getting married, asking who had my sister in a lip lock on the dock at the lake—a guy no one's seen before. And of course I'm like, yeah, you're full of shit, but then, nope, he's right, because next text is a photo of you and this guy, lips glued together, his tongue down your throat and his hands on your ass."

She just glanced over to Paige, who had her hand on the top of her compact, then over to her dad and older brother, Gabriel, now walking their way from the barn. She took another step toward the porch. Jeremy was holding out his phone, and the image of her in a kiss with that damn handsome stranger was on the screen. For a second, she couldn't pull her eyes from that photo, from the horror of seeing the attractive guy holding her closer than she'd remembered. In fact, it seemed as if she couldn't get close enough to him, considering, in that photo, her arms were around his shoulders and neck as he held her, skin to skin, so close there was no mistaking the intimacy between them. The only problem was it was all a lie.

She said nothing as she flicked her gaze up to her brother, who knew her better than anyone. "It's not what it seems, and you can't tell anyone. And since when are you still friends with Kurt?"

Jeremy lifted his soda and took a swallow, flicking his gaze over to her dad. He pocketed his phone.

Chelsea could hear her dad and Gabriel, laughing and talking about something she couldn't make out. They were both in faded blue jeans covered in dust and grit, and they looked as if they'd rolled in a pile of dirt. Her dad wore a blue shirt with the sleeves rolled up, and Gabriel was in a black and white T-shirt, a ballcap over his dark hair.

"Kurt's a dick, but at least I know what's happening with you and with everyone," Jeremy whispered. "Also heard that Boone was messing with you again. Just say the word and I'll talk with him."

She knew her brother would do more than that. He wouldn't stop with just a word. It would involve his temper, his fists, and then her dad would find out, and then her parents would be involved. To make it worse, then they'd find out everything she didn't want anyone to know. This was her problem, hers alone to solve.

"You promised me you wouldn't say anything, Jeremy, and I'm holding you to that promise. Leave it alone. Besides, that stranger may have just—"

"Any gas left in my truck?" her dad, Andy Friessen, called out as he strode up to the house. His short dark hair was threaded with more gray these days, she noticed. As she stared over to her dad, she couldn't figure out what to say. He raised a brow, his intense gaze softening as it landed on her. She tossed the truck keys, and her dad caught them with one hand.

"Lots," she said. "Just went to the lake and back. Couldn't find the time to fit in any joyriding."

Her dad rested his foot on the bottom step, giving her a teasing look. Gabriel said something to Paige that had her laughing as she yanked open the door of her car, and the door hinge squeaked again.

"Gotta go, girl! Call me later," Paige called out. "Bye, Mr. Friessen!"

Her dad turned and lifted his hand as Paige slid behind the wheel of her car and fired up the twenty-year-old compact, which rattled and rumbled. "She needs to get that car looked at, Chelsea," Andy said.

Chelsea just shrugged, knowing next time her friend came out, her dad was likely to pop the hood and take a look for himself. "It still runs," she said, turning her gaze back to her brother and staring at him, hoping he wouldn't say anything.

"So what's going on?" Andy said as he looked from her to Jeremy, who shrugged and lifted his soda to take another swallow. His expression let on nothing. She realized then that her brother had the same poker face as her dad. It was so unnerving at times.

"Chelsea was just filling me in on her day at the lake," Jeremy finally said, and she glared daggers at him, knowing he loved stirring everything up. Then a slow smile touched his lips. "But you know Chelsea. She likely had her head buried in a book most of the day."

The way her dad looked from her to Jeremy, she wondered if he knew more or wondered what they were hiding. Could he read their minds?

"You forget to tell us something?" came a voice from behind them. The screen door squeaked, and Laura Friessen stepped out. Her mom's long blond hair was piled up in a messy bun, and she was barefoot in a jean skirt and pink and white sleeveless blouse, holding the cordless phone. Her green eyes were flashing with a fire Chelsea didn't see often in her mom, so she just looked to Jeremy, who said nothing. She still couldn't get her tongue to move.

"It seems our daughter forgot to tell us some very important news," Laura said, "which it seems the entire county already knows! So when were you planning on telling your father and me? We are your parents, and news of this magnitude, I'd have thought—no, expected you to tell us first."

"Oh, shit," she thought she heard Jeremy say. Gabriel stepped around her dad, and everyone was staring down at her.

"What news? Chels, what's going on?" Andy said. He had a way of asking that let her know there wasn't a snowball's chance in hell she could sneak off without answering. This was it.

She opened her mouth, about to say, "What?" But all that came out was air, a mere squeak, and she found herself looking over to Jeremy again. She needed him to come up with something, anything, that would save her from having to explain what she hoped her mom hadn't really heard anything about.

"It seems she's getting married. Is that about right, Chelsea?" The way her mom said it, she knew her wishful thinking was about to die a slow death. Her dad stared up at her mom and then turned his icy blue eyes her way. Once he learned what had really happened, she'd no longer be able to keep from him the one thing she'd hidden from everyone, which was what had really happened between her and Boone and the humiliation she'd continued to endure for the last two years, all because of what she'd discovered.

"It's not really true." Boy, did that sound weak. She cleared her throat.

Her dad lifted a brow, and she pulled in a breath, looking up to Jeremy again, who'd been sworn to secrecy.

"Then explain it, Chelsea," Andy said, "because that doesn't cut it. Either it's true or it isn't. So why is it that your mother and the county are under the impression you're getting married?"

Gabriel appeared confused, looking from her to their mom and dad, only her dad wasn't looking away. Her mom was still holding the phone, waiting for her to answer. She once again felt as if she'd been suddenly thrust under a microscope, and for a second, she didn't think it could get any worse.

"Because of a kiss from a total stranger who saved me from embarrassment," she blurted out.

There, she'd said it. Problem solved. Only, as she watched the exchange between her mom and dad and the way Jeremy and Gabriel stared at her as if she'd lost her mind, she knew this wasn't going to be the end of it.

About the Author

"Lorhainne Eckhart is one of my go to authors when I want a guaranteed good book. So many twists and turns, but also so much love and such a strong sense of family."

(Lora W., Reviewer)

New York Times & USA Today bestseller Lorhainne Eckhart writes Raw Relatable Real Romance is best known for her big family romances series, where "Morals and family are running themes. Danger, romance, and a drive to do what is right will see you glued to the page." As one fan calls her, she is the "Queen of the family saga." (aherman) writing "the ups and downs of what goes on within a family but also with some suspense, angst and of course a bit of romance thrown in for good measure." Follow Lorhainne on Bookbub to receive alerts on New Releases and Sales and join her mailing list at LorhainneEckhart.com for her Monday Blog, books news, giveaways and FREE reads. With over 120 books, audiobooks, and multiple series published and available at all retailers now translated into six languages. She is a multiple recipient of the Readers' Favorite Award for Suspense and Romance, and lives in the Pacific Northwest on an island, is the mother of three, her oldest has autism and she is an advocate for never giving up on your dreams.

"Lorhainne Eckhart has this uncanny way of just hitting the spot every time with her books."

(Caroline L., Reviewer)

The O'Connells: *The O'Connells of Livingston, Montana are not your typical family. A riveting collection of stories surrounding the ups and downs of what goes on within a family but also with some suspense, angst and of course a bit of romance thrown in for good measure "I thought I loved the Friessens, but I absolutely adore the O'Connell's. Each and every book has totally different genres of stories but the one thing in common is how she is able to wrap it around the family which is the heart of each story." (C. Logue)*

The Friessens: *An emotional big family romance series, the Friessen family siblings find their relationships tested, lay their hearts on the line, and discover lasting love! "Lorhainne Eckhart is one of my go to authors when I want a guaranteed good book. So many twists and turns, but also so much love and such a strong sense of family." (Lora W., Reviewer)*

The Parker Sisters: *The Parker Sisters are a close-knit family, and like any other family they have their ups and downs. "Eckhart has crafted another intense family drama…The character development is outstanding, and the emotional investment is high…" (Aherman, Reviewer)*

The McCabe Brothers: *Join the five McCabe siblings on their journeys to the dark and dangerous side of love! An intense, exhilarating collection of romantic thrillers you won't want to miss. — "Eckhart has a new series that is definitely worth the read. The queen of the family saga started this series with a spin-off of her wildly successful Friessen series." From a Readers' Favorite award—winning author and "queen of the family saga" (Aherman)*

Lorhainne loves to hear from her readers! You can connect with me at:
www.LorhainneEckhart.com
lorhainneeckhart.le@gmail.com

The Outsider Series
The Forgotten Child (Brad and Emily)
A Baby and a Wedding *(An Outsider Series Short)*
Fallen Hero (Andy, Jed, and Diana)
The Search *(An Outsider Series Short)*
The Awakening (Andy and Laura)
Secrets (Jed and Diana)
Runaway (Andy and Laura)
Overdue *(An Outsider Series Short)*
The Unexpected Storm (Neil and Candy)
The Wedding (Neil and Candy)

The Friessens: A New Beginning
The Deadline (Andy and Laura)
The Price to Love (Neil and Candy)
A Different Kind of Love (Brad and Emily)
A Vow of Love, A Friessen Family Christmas

The Friessens
The Reunion
The Bloodline (Andy & Laura)
The Promise (Diana & Jed)
The Business Plan (Neil & Candy)
The Decision (Brad & Emily)
First Love (Katy)
Family First
Leave the Light On
In the Moment
In the Family

In the Silence
In the Charm
Unexpected Consequences
It Was Always You
The First Time I Saw You
Welcome to My Arms
Welcome to Boston
I'll Always Love You
Ground Rules
A Reason to Breathe
You Are My Everything
Anything For You
The Homecoming
Stay Away From My Daughter
The Bad Boy
A Place of Our Own
The Visitor
All About Devon
Long Past Dawn
How to Heal a Heart
Keep Me In Your Heart

The O'Connells
The Neighbor
The Third Call
The Secret Husband
The Quiet Day
The Commitment
The Missing Father
The Hometown Hero
Justice
The Family Secret
The Fallen O'Connell
The Return of the O'Connells

And The She Was Gone
The Stalker
The O'Connell Family Christmas
The Girl Next Door
Broken Promises
The Gatekeeper

The McCabe Brothers
Don't Stop Me (Vic)
Don't Catch Me (Chase)
Don't Run From Me (Aaron)
Don't Hide From Me (Luc)
Don't Leave Me (Claudia)
Out of Time

A Billy Jo McCabe Mystery
Nothing As it Seems
Hiding in Plain Sight
The Cold Case
The Trap
Above the Law
The Stranger at the Door
The Children

The Wilde Brothers
The One (Joe and Margaret)
The Honeymoon, A Wilde Brothers Short
Friendly Fire (Logan and Julia)
Not Quite Married, A Wilde Brothers Short
A Matter of Trust (Ben and Carrie)
The Reckoning, A Wilde Brothers Christmas
Traded (Jake)
Unforgiven (Samuel)
The Holiday Bride

Married in Montana
His Promise
Love's Promise
A Promise of Forever

The Parker Sisters
Thrill of the Chase
The Dating Game
Play Hard to Get
What We Can't Have
Go Your Own Way
A June Wedding

Kate & Walker
One Night
Edge of Night
Last Night

Walk the Right Road Series
The Choice
Lost and Found
Merkaba
Bounty
Blown Away: The Final Chapter

The Saved Series
Saved
Vanished
Captured

Single Titles
He Came Back
Loving Christine

For my German Readers
Die Außenseiter-Reihe
Der Vergessene Junge
Der Gefallene Held

For my French Readers
L'ENFANT OUBLIÉ